A Seal *of* Salvage

CLAYTON B. SMITH

BREAKWATER
P.O. Box 2188, St. John's, NL, Canada, A1C 6E6
WWW.BREAKWATERBOOKS.COM

COPYRIGHT © 2024 Clayton B. Smith
COVER ILLUSTRATION © 2024 Noah Bender
ISBN 9781778530104 (softcover)

A CIP catalogue record for this book is available from Library and Archives Canada.

ALL RIGHTS RESERVED. No part of this publication may be reproduced, stored in a retrieval system or transmitted, in any form or by any means, without the prior written consent of the publisher or a licence from the Canadian Copyright Licensing Agency (Access Copyright). For an Access Copyright licence, visit www.accesscopyright.ca or call toll free 1-800-893-5777.

We acknowledge the support of the Canada Council for the Arts. We acknowledge the financial support of the Government of Canada through the Department of Heritage and the Government of Newfoundland and Labrador through the Department of Tourism, Culture, Arts and Recreation for our publishing activities.

PRINTED AND BOUND IN CANADA.

Canada Council for the Arts Conseil des arts du Canada

Newfoundland Labrador

This book is printed on a recycled paper and other controlled sources that are certified by the Forest Stewardship Council®.

For those who dare to love.

Salvage

A town located on the Eastport Peninsula of Bonavista Bay, in the Canadian province of Newfoundland and Labrador.

The story of Oliver Brown once lingered around the town of Salvage. Often, when the story had been told over kitchen tables, over mugs of white tea with breath of black rum, it would become magical in the most terrible sort of way. But it's a story of yesterday; it's of yesterday's ways and yesterday's beliefs. Some tales stand longer than their times, of course, but this isn't one of them. It's faded more than the oldest wharves, and its tellings are as few as there are fish in the harbour.

You won't struggle to hear a yarn about Oliver Brown. But to hear the true story is more of an endeavour. Down the end of Main Street, there's a saltbox that's lasted a full century, and in it lives the widow Rebecca Genge. If, for some reason, you fancy hearing the story of Oliver's time in Salvage, Mrs. Genge is who you should find. She knew him for a short time, you see. Not well enough to think that she deserves to be called his friend, but well enough that, by the end, he might have called her one. Mrs. Genge is known to be a storyteller, the type only her generation could ever produce. A teller of stories littered with inconsequential characters and riddled with inconsistencies, but always close enough to being plausible and anchored in just enough of reality that you can't help but anxiously await every word. She never let the story of Oliver run away. He'd saved her husband's life—at least once, for certain—so perhaps she felt she owed it to him to keep the tale honest.

The story begins before Oliver had ever been thought of, as many of these stories do. Although Rebecca was even further from being a consideration, she has asked enough questions of enough people over the years that at least a gesturing towards the truth has been compiled. It's a story's beginning that Oliver himself was told on a stormy night, when he was only a boy.

These days, few of the folk who try to tell the tale can agree on what the cause for the party was. What all these storytellers are consistent about is that everyone in the town had been aware of the disappearance of Stella's dress. Some will include in their stories the size of the full moon, or the sudden strength of the northeast gale. Some will say the moon was bright enough that it could have been midday at midnight, while others will claim that there was no moon at all, and the fog was so thick you couldn't count your own fingers.

According to Mrs. Genge, though, the moon was not full, nor was it new. It was an obscure moon giving half-colours to "quarter-things." It offered some guidance, but one still had to be careful getting home. The fog had settled late and just offshore, and the boats were all in long before it blanketed the harbour. Mrs. Genge believes that the night was that of Robert Feltham's wedding. Feltham was the mayor of Salvage and had been for some time. All of the town, half of the next two coves, and a fair portion of the next bay had been there for the occasion.

And despite the claims of every storyteller, not one of the souls in the church hall that night, including Stella herself, had any idea that her dress hadn't been on the line when she'd taken her clothes in that afternoon.

Albert Brown sat with a small collection of companions: his friend, Dorman; his uncle by marriage, Aubrey; and his cousin Sandy, who was perched on the lap of another friend, Colin. Albert hadn't settled into his drink yet. It was early for the night of a party, but despite his youth, he had already found a fancy for the bottoms of glasses. His companions saw the look in his eye and the corner of his mouth twisting into a grin. He intended to enjoy himself, that much is true. The innocence of Albert's intentions, or the ignorance of his actions; well, that part even Mrs. Genge isn't quite sure of. Maybe that look in his eye is precisely the reason that his was the gaze she caught, or maybe it has nothing to do with the story at all.

Now, over cups of English Breakfast before bed, and in hushed tones beneath raised eyebrows, it will always be said that the unfamiliar woman walked through the church hall and straight up to Albert's chair. Some will add that she attracted the eyes of two dozen men and a dozen women, only half of the total married, when she parted the crowd. But in truth, she lingered quietly by the door for some time. Despite the beauty of her awestruck smile, the excitement in her eyes, and the way that her dress fell a little too high on her thighs, she was barely even noticed.

Albert saw her immediately, though. There was no parting of the people, but he caught glimpses of her as the crowd swelled and shifted and rolled with the music, her face appearing and disappearing over shoulders and between bodies.

"Who's that?" he'd asked no one in particular, without turning his head towards his friends.

Aubrey thought he was talking about Mary Glover, dancing in the corner with Clarke Genge. Dorman barely heard Albert's words; he was too caught up staring at Stella. Colin and Sandy had hardly looked past each other's lips in three quarters less an hour.

Albert asked again and received only the band's continuous reply.

"Dorman," Albert shouted. "Who's that then?" he asked for the third time, with a jerk of his head towards the door.

All the folks around the table turned to look then, gawking more blatantly than they realized. Not one of them could put a name to the face. None of them could even take a guess at who she was related to. Her features were too different, too smooth, too soft.

Sandy quickly grew excited. She wasn't used to seeing her cousin's heart in his eyes. She thought she'd ask around. Dorman said they'd both see her better through another beer; Albert wasn't the type to decline such a suggestion. But he still only offered a nod, scared to take his eyes away from the door, not wanting the woman to get lost in the sea of people.

Now a couple young men did make an attempt at speaking to her, but it wasn't with lips soaked in lust the way the story is so often told. Some ladies even offered polite hellos, for she didn't hold the intimidating beauty that's so often claimed. No, she was always approachable, only striking once you'd taken the time to look at her.

Now, people attribute it to the drink, but it was just as much the times that gave Albert the courage it took to ask her to dance. To hear it told, Albert must have been heir to half of England, the way the girls looked after him when he walked across the dance floor. But in truth, he wasn't any better off than any other fisherman who kept port in Salvage, and the ladies in attendance weren't so naive as to think otherwise, or shallow enough to care in either case. But that didn't keep jealousy from sharpening tongues in years to come.

Whether it was due to jealousy or just curiosity, when Albert crossed the room and asked the woman—who couldn't be recognized as from anywhere along the shore—if she'd join him in a dance, there weren't many folks who didn't take notice.

When Albert took her in his arms, and the band began playing to the rhythm of their feet, her beauty was inescapable. The joy in her laugh was infectious, and the entire room began to smile. Albert found himself falling into eyes so many leagues deep that he never did surface again. And through the entrancement on his face, the room saw her beauty for themselves: the spacing of her freckles, the curls of her hair, the distinction of her dimples—and the way that the swing of her hips, which barely swung, left even the bishop wiping his brow. She was the moonlight through stained glass, the space between the fiddle and the shanty, the calm between rolling breaths.

Oh, she captured that party. She was so unforgettable that she was the only part of the night that became ingrained in the collective memory of the harbour. So incredible was she that no one was surprised when, only two fortnights later, a crowd of smaller yet not insulting size gathered for the wedding of Albert and the woman called Georgia.

No one seems to recall why she had no family in attendance. Nor does anyone try to claim that they'd asked her. She had a story, more plausible than it was impossible, that kept questions on tips of tongues and not asked aloud. But there were darting glances and eyes on shoes even then.

The wedding hadn't been a year in memory when a child was born. Thick, curly black hair and eyes that quickly turned to a deep brown. It was the mother's child. The child didn't see its first birthday before the consumption came to the town. Albert was forced to leave the home before the babe had babbled any derivation of "dad." He was taken aboard a quarantine ship for the sake of townsfolk and kin. Shortly after the baby's first birthday, a letter came via the M/V *Christmas Seal*, informing Georgia that her husband hadn't woken. It wasn't long afterwards that they were found in the house. The child doesn't remember it, but he was found with his mother. Standing on top of her cold body in a bathtub of salt water, the child was clinging to life, too tired to even cry.

No one took full responsibility for the depth of the grave. But the child was young and healthy, and it was Albert's Aunt Elizabeth, Aubrey's wife, who took it upon herself to claim responsibility for the youngster. She hadn't needed to, she would always say, but she had offered none the less. She left out that she had offered before it needed to be asked aloud so that others wouldn't need to find reasons to say no, and things that no one wished to address could be left unsaid.

The next few years hold little to tell as, day by day, a baby becomes a person. And parentage aside, the person is what makes the story of Oliver Brown one worth telling.

Baccalao

Salted and/or dried codfish.

The soft stones have given way along the coast of Bonavista Bay. The shoreline now is either enduring or eroding: sharp cliffs or pebbled beaches that break the waves as they're formed by them. There are faces on the shoreline that feel as unforgiving as they look. There are fingers that reach so far out the sea has tamed them until smooth. There are rocks that the water has long since enveloped that still linger just a swell away from the surface. There are things off this shoreline that humans haven't yet pulled from the sea. There are humans along that shoreline, perpetually pulled by the sea.

Oliver Brown, a boy no more than nine, lay on a smooth seaside rock. He lay on his back with arms outstretched and legs spread; he was entirely naked, exposed to sea and sky. His eyes were closed as he absorbed the summer sun that had warmed his rock. Curly, black hair was painted to his forehead. The sun, filtered through patchy grey skies, slowly pulled the sea water from his skin, frizzing his hair and leaving a dusty white residue.

He rolled over with exaggerated effort, sleepily enjoying the cold Atlantic evaporating off him. The air was almost still; no wind threatened to steal his shirt away from where it hung on the alder bushes. There wasn't even enough breeze to ruffle his hair.

No day is calm enough to stop the lapping of the ocean, though. The boy listened as the water clapped, falling upon the lowest rocks and splashing against the sides of larger ones. The ocean seemed gentle, the waves barely there; but when he'd been swimming, Oliver had felt a fullness to the seas. The waves didn't lazily meet the shoreline; they didn't roll past him with indifference. Instead, the ocean seemed heavy, forceful. The swell wasn't large, but it was firm. He'd felt it in his chest with every pass. The boy enjoyed the force of the ocean on his little body; the power engulfed him, like a hug that didn't let go. But it had seemed unsettled today, its rhythm more emphatic than soothing.

In the distance, seagulls were screeching a call to arms. When they got closer, he'd need to get dressed and make his way back towards the town. The seagulls would follow the fishing boats in, hover above in clouds with size and volume reflecting a fisherman's fortune. When Oliver hears the gulls' calls grow closer, he'll know the boats aren't far from rounding the point. He clings to the rock while he can, enjoying the moment. He doesn't manage to get all the way out to this point every day. And some days, even when he does, the ocean is striking the shoreline hard enough that it keeps him from wetting his toes.

In the distance he could hear the waves at Broomclose Head. The ocean is deep there, right up to the land, and the swell comes straight in, unbroken by the Shag Islands or Little Denier. The headland is almost sheer, and the water breaks upon it with sounds as sharp as slate. Caves are carved into Broomclose, giant caves. As the swell grows, those caves let out a mighty thundering. Every collision of ocean and rock is echoed and amplified, projected out in a deafening warning.

The distant boom of Broomclose is just a drumbeat. Oliver has felt his own heart beat against the rocks and has imagined it matching the rolling waves. It never has, of course, but he wishes that it would.

A sharp cracking sound, just three feet from his head, snapped the boy's eyes open. The shattered body of a large crab was broken open on the rock next to him, dropped from the sky to expose the meat. Just as Oliver took in the splattered form across the rock, he heard the shrill call of the gull above him, unhappy that someone was so near its lunch. He looked back at the crab; its dark shell was broken all the way around, and its body seeped out from the cracks. Cold insides, little more than liquid, dribbled their way down the rock. The crab was big, too big to linger in the shallows where the gull could reach it. It must have been pulled up in a fisherman's nets.

Oliver jumped to his feet.

A seagull wouldn't carry its catch further than it needed to. The boat that had thrown the crab overside had to be close. Oliver hadn't heard any approaching cacophony of gulls' grating voices and fishermen bellowing over them that would have signalled a good catch, so he feared that the fishing hadn't been good.

He jumped over the seagull's shattered meal and left the wet imprint of his skin upon the rock. He pulled his trousers and shirt from their hanging place on the alder bush. Cotton stuck to his skin as he tried to force his feet through the pant legs; he was still too wet to be getting dressed. Sticking his socks in his pockets and jamming his shirt through his belt loop, he stole a glance over his shoulder, towards the point. The ocean seemed to be growing darker, but its ripples and waves weren't caused by anything he could see. He climbed up from the rocky shoreline and through the alder bushes, pushing his way towards the stunted fir trees.

Oliver followed the coast back to the harbour, as much as he could. He tried to keep the water in sight, and he tried to keep out of sight of the water. He skirted the scattered stilted homes that stretch farthest down the shore. As he got further into the harbour town, he was forced deeper into the trees, trying his hardest to avoid encountering anyone. The goowiddy got thicker and he lifted his legs higher, making large, slow steps through the undergrowth. The leafy bog bushes left scratches on his ankles, bare between shoe and pant leg, reminding him of the socks balled up in his pockets. Little leaves and fallen needles stuck to his damp skin.

The ground began to get steeper as Oliver climbed the hills that surrounded the harbour. Creeping higher, moving continually away from the ocean, he looked down upon the collection of colours that made up the town he was raised in. Houses in dark reds and bright yellows, haphazardly placed around the cove. From his vantage point, he could see his aunt and uncle's house. He could have gotten to it in half the time if he'd taken the shore. Continuing his journey, he cut crosswise along the hillside, a gull's lazy swoop around a harbour free of fish.

When he'd made his way far enough around the cove, Oliver perched himself upon a rock. It was large and flat and mismatched with its surroundings, a glacial dropping on the hillside. But it wasn't as smooth as his seaside sunbed. Pulling his socks from his pockets, and brushing the forest from his feet, he looked down at the white boats beginning to trail into the harbour. As he watched the wooden frames returning, he knew the path they would take, cutting across the harbour mouth at an angle and then turning sharp to port, another three boat lengths and then a hard starboard. The mouth of the harbour seemed wide enough that the boats could make it in abeam of each other. But off one point stretched a shoal, bare and jagged at low tide, hidden by only a foot of water when the tide was in. There were rocks and deadheads too, none of which posed the slightest danger to the fisherman familiar with them, but all together creating an unseen route into the harbour.

Oliver watched them on their way in, heel to keel, a meandering line of white ducks with bold black numbers, declaring on their sides their right to fish. The boats were coming in all at once. The boy wondered for a moment if this meant the fish were good, and the fishermen all wanted to make it out again. But too much of the gunwales rose above the water; the boats were coming in light. The fish weren't good, so maybe the weather was even worse.

Oliver didn't yet understand the forces that could swirl far out, where the inshore boats could never reach. He didn't know of the warning the swell could give if it beat the storm to shore. He hadn't come to fear the ocean, perhaps he never would, but he'd come to understand why others did. In that moment, with socks pulled up over scratched ankles and a wrinkled shirt tugged from belt loop and hauled over damp hair, Oliver found the boats coming in early an exciting event. An irregularity that intrigued him.

The wharves that lined the harbour were hidden from Oliver's view; the houses and the sharp slope down to the water left the moorings all hidden. Oliver was about to lose sight of the first of the boats as they came into the harbour. He couldn't yet make out his uncle's boat, and he knew he'd lose sight of them all as he descended the hill.

The goowiddy was thick on the hillside, and there were alders woven tight together wherever stunted trees weren't, but it was all downhill. He could make it, he thought, if he went straight down through the trees. He could beat the last of the boats to the wharves.

Oliver leapt from his dressing rock and began his way down in great bounding steps. He let gravity do half of his work in the reckless manner only children can fully embrace. His limbs fought to keep pace with the speed of his falling. He was excited by the moment, by the event of everyone returning all at once, and now he was excited by nothing other than his free fall down the hillside. He held his hands up in front of him, not worrying about the scratches caused by branches but not wanting to lose his eye to one either. He closed his eyes entirely for a moment, hoping for even footing and continuing without breaking his pace.

All at once the trees stopped, and the boy almost tripped as he was forced to jump over the deep troughs of Missy Smith's potato garden. He ran around to the front of Missy's house and then took a left down the road. The house he lived in, his aunt and uncle's white two-storey with the red trim around every window, was only fifty yards further down the road. He'd cut straight through their garden and down towards the wharf, and he'd beat his uncle there. He wore anticipation on his face, a smile from ear to ear. He had an image of himself standing on the very end of the wharf. His uncle could toss the painter—the rope attached to the bow of the boat—up to him, and Oliver would help pull the boat in. The men would hand him up their gear, and he'd be a great help, bringing it all in off the wharf while they unloaded the heavy tubs of their catch.

The boy didn't go through the gate of his aunt's garden. He jumped clear over the little fence with a hoot and a laugh. He hadn't broken pace since he'd left the rock back up the hill, and now he was almost there.

"Oliver Brown!"

The boy stopped in his tracks. His feet planted so hard that his momentum almost made him tumble over. He contemplated pretending that he hadn't heard her even though he'd already stopped, but the potential of a scolding kept him still.

Oliver looked out at the harbour. The boats had dispersed from their parade in; almost all had reached their respective wharves.

"Where've you gotten yourself to all day?" his aunt shouted, louder than the distance required.

"Nowhere, Aunt Elizabeth."

"Yes, I'm sure. And while you've been out galivanting around nowhere, doing nothing, I've been stuck here, doing your chores."

Oliver heard the outer door of the house close, a hard-cracking sound of wood against wood. His aunt was a formidable woman, in character as well as form. She took the steps down from the porch to the yard gingerly. You'd be tempted to think she's slow from the way that she chose her steps leaving the house. But once her feet were on the lawn, she crossed from one side to the other quicker than a scald cat. Oliver turned to see his aunt standing over him.

"Where do you think you're off to now in such a hurry?"

"The wharf! They're all on the way in—"

"I'm not blind, b'y. I sees where the boats are to just as well as you do. I don't understand what difference that makes to you is all."

"I'm going to help Uncle Aub unload—"

"You think the men need the help of your little arms?"

"I could lay out some fish, or I can help untangle the lines." He held up his hands as if showcasing his dexterity, his usefulness.

"Lay the fish out? Do you think they'll be 'tall concerned with laying fish out here this afternoon?"

"Well—"

"You think yer uncle is gonna come back round the point, this time a day, and 'ave near enough fish that needs be laid out?" She shook her head and her jowls jiggled. "No, my son, I tell you. Only reason he'd be coming back now is if the gunwales were about to go under 'cause she's filled to the brim, or 'cause a storm's brewin'. And you can read those gunwales, can't ya?"

Oliver kept his head down.

"*Can't* ya!"

He nodded emphatically. "Well, I can help them pull her up the slip or—"

"I dare say, too. You'd be tripped over enough times they'd need to tie you down as well as their gear. What about that wood you was supposed to bring in the s'marnin?"

"I brought in half a cord before I left."

"And what about the other half a cord then?"

"There's almost no more split up."

"Boy, stop arguing with me and go get at the wood. If you gets enough done before your uncle comes up to the house, I'll let you on your way again before supper."

Oliver sighed and stopped arguing. Despite her severity, his aunt was being kind to him, and he didn't want to push his luck. He began walking towards the wood shed at the back of the house.

As he walked by, Elizabeth reached out and patted his head. The second time palm touched hair, it didn't leave. Her fingers gripped onto his curls, and she pulled him back with a hard jerk. Oliver let out a howl. The hand let go of his hair only long enough to grab his ear. She twisted the cartilage so hard that Oliver knew he could feel the skin being pulled apart.

"Oliver Brown, you tell me right now why your hair is sodden wet."

Oliver opened his mouth.

Aunt Elizabeth twisted his ear even harder. "I'll pull this ear right off yer head if you even thinks about lying to me."

He closed his mouth and opened it again.

She twisted even harder. "And if you tells me you've been swimming, I'll skin ya."

Oliver closed his mouth once more. Unsure if it was better to lose an ear or one's skin.

"I was up the pond," he said.

He had come down the hill, near the pond. And he hadn't swum in the pond, but he hadn't said he had been swimming in the—

Oliver's aunt grabbed his face, chin in the crook between forefinger and thumb. She released his ear and licked her thumb, rubbing it hard along Oliver's cheek from temple to jawline. The friction burned and Oliver wondered if this is how you start to skin someone. When she pulled away, a white residue of salt powdered her thumb.

"You was up the pond. You're as salt as the baccalao, and yer tellin' me you was up the pond." She wiped the salt away on her apron as if it was some kind of foul substance. "You must think I'm some stupid." She let go of Oliver's chin with a raise of her hand, cocking his head backward, almost pushing him over.

Oliver looked at his feet, face burning from more than her grip. He opened his mouth, about to apologize, or defend himself, or the ocean, or all the above, and she raised her hand. It was straight up in front of her, like she was signalling for him to stop, and then it turned just a hair, telling him what she'd do if he didn't.

"You say nudding. Chop wood."

~

Oliver's shirt had barely dried of sea water when sweat began to soak through it. He leaned onto an axe, almost as tall as him, breathing hard. All the boats had long since been secured in the harbour. Most were pulled onto shore for the night, tied tightly even then. Fishermen were still on the beach, checking lines and tying down gear. Oliver's cheeks were sharp red, from the wind as much as the effort. Wood chips, bark and branches were beginning to be picked up by the storm and whipped through the air. The patchwork sunlight that had warmed his seaside rock only an hour before was now lost behind a dark and smouldering sky.

To have a good winter, you need to think about it all spring and all summer. Oliver had been told this many times over, whenever he questioned how desperately chores needed to be done. Every action now is a salvation for later. Oliver tried to gain satisfaction from the importance for the future, but he was still too much a child to imagine the winter's cold when the wood ran out. He couldn't think of the danger in bottles of food running low, or snow refusing to melt, or sea ice packing the harbour for weeks on end. And so he did chores because he was told, not because he knew them to be necessary.

The wood was always the worst, both to him and on him. His aunt said that his skin was too soft for a boy his age. Underworked and needed to be toughened up, she said. As Oliver felt his palm blister from the smooth-handled axe and then tear open against the rough bark of a spruce junk, he had little faith in chopping wood ever being easier.

The weather kept coming up. Oliver turned junks too large to pile into splits and then piled all the wood, piece by piece, in the shed behind the house. The wood itself wasn't as heavy as it could be. Cut last year, it had dried for a summer and a winter and another summer still. But Oliver's arms were thin, like the rest of him, and it didn't take long for the work to become a struggle.

By the time his uncle Aubrey came up over the hill to the yard, the sun had all but given up on breaking through the clouds above Salvage. The wind had whistled itself into a deafening howl. Oliver had his back to the water while he worked. He didn't see his uncle look into the wood shed at the freshly stowed pile, stacked higher than the boy's head. Aubrey came up behind the swinging axe; he watched it go down, driven only by its weight. He watched the boy's trembling hands then, trying to pull it free from the block.

"That's enough, I'd say."

Oliver didn't hesitate in putting down the axe. He was shameless in cupping his hands but didn't make a show of it. He refused to look at them, instead turning and looking up at his uncle Aubrey's bright eyes hidden behind dark brows and a heavy beard. The kindness there was hard to make out.

Aubrey turned the boy around and guided him by the shoulder towards the house, a slow and steady pace. The wooden door was already open, Elizabeth looking on.

"He hasn't been at that for half as long as he's told you!" she called.

Aubrey didn't say anything but continued walking towards the door.

"There's well more to be done outdoors."

"Nah, Liza, we're done for the day now." Aubrey moved his hand to the boy's back and pushed him onwards.

"Dinner will be a while yet, and there's lots of daylight left! You come in and sit down and leave the boy to work."

"Get the boy a cup of tea. I'll be in now the once."

"A cup of tea? Sure, he only just got home. I don't see why he needs—"

"Cup of tea." Aubrey took a pipe from his breast pocket and turned away from his wife.

"Aubrey!" She hissed his name, like she was screaming in a hush.

He turned slightly and eyed her.

"The boy's been out in the water, Aub." A hot whisper. She looked towards Oliver, not to him, just around him, as if he were a wound beginning to fester.

Aubrey turned all the way around. He pulled the pipe from his mouth. He exhaled—not a sigh, a deep breath—and knelt down in front of the boy.

"Is that right?" he said.

Oliver stared at the goowiddy still stuck to the rolled cotton of his socks.

Aubrey turned his head down at an angle until he caught the boy's eyes. Oliver tried to hold the gaze, tried to match the tight-lipped expression, but his bottom lip couldn't help but tremble.

"Were you swimming?" Aubrey said softly.

Oliver hesitated and then nodded, quick and slight. He opened his mouth.

"Don't let him tell you that he was up in the pond—"

Aubrey raised his hand up, straight and open towards his wife, and didn't move his gaze from Oliver's. The boy's eyes were big and brown and welled up.

"Oliver, did anyone see you when you were swimming, or when you were on the shore?"

"No, sir." It was little more than a squeak, shaking the whole way through.

"You're sure?"

Oliver nodded and swallowed deep. He blinked twice, three times, quickly.

Aubrey rose from his crouched position and put his pipe back to his mouth. "Go on inside." He gave a wave away with his hand. "Rinse yer hands good. Aunt Elizabeth will get you an early tea."

Elizabeth stood staring at her husband, face greyer than the old sun-bleached wharf, as the boy moved past her and inside.

"There's a storm coming," Aubrey said.

"Aye, I can tell from the howl and the empty boat—"

"Bobby Ryan went out beyond the third shoal this morning." He lit his pipe with a match that seemed too small for the size of his hands. "Put the kettle on. I told May that she could come by."

Aubrey wasn't looking to see Elizabeth's face change. He was staring out past the harbour to a place that eyes can't reach.

"If he's careful coming, he'll make it in, in a good few hours. Or in the morning, if he finds shore somewhere else." Aubrey took two long steps back towards the wharf and then stopped. He watched as the wind took the heads off whitecaps, spraying sheets along the harbour.

"Put the kettle on," he said, without turning back to the door.

Flipsy

To jump or traverse from one ice pan to another.

Two years after the storm that Bobby Ryan hadn't beaten to shore, spring came all at once. It had been a hard winter, and the improvement of the weather was regarded warily.

"Only thing worse than a late spring is a false one," Aunt Elizabeth said, standing at the kitchen window. Hands on hips, she clenched her jaw as she looked out over the ice-encrusted town. She warned of trusting the change. She'd seen Aprils as hard as Februaries and preached that bottles of provisions should still be counted and the fire stoked only when the house was shivering.

Oliver didn't take much heed in her warning; to him, spring was clearly here. When he stood outside, he could feel the sunshine on his skin. That was winter's end to him: when the sun could be felt as well as seen.

Oliver hated the winter. The weather had kept him captive inside the house. Going out required at least one pair of long johns, two pairs of his thickest wool socks, and as many shirts and sweaters as his aunt could force over his head. Oliver didn't understand the need of being so overdressed; the cold never caught his bones the way his aunt claimed it could. But Elizabeth insisted that he dress up just as well as the other children despite his protests. The trouble it took to go outdoors didn't allow for leisurely winter walks, as his aunt would engage in the layering only so he could make the hike to school.

Once, before Christmas, Oliver had taken the long way back from school. He had wandered along the shoreline, breaking ice from the rocks, climbing over the ballicatters and making paths in the snow. By the time he'd returned home, he'd soaked through every stitch of clothing he had on. Elizabeth had cursed him continuously as she laid his clothing over the wood stove. Aubrey had to add another junk of wood to the fire just so Oliver would have something to wear the next day. He'd received a tanning that warmed his bottom better than his long johns, and he took only the most direct routes back and forth to the schoolhouse after that day. Elizabeth had made Aubrey deliver the spanking. When it was through and Oliver's eyes were full but not leaking, Aubrey had told him, "Clothes come dry, after long enough. But if your body gets too wet and cold, there's not enough heat in the house to ever get it gone."

Oliver had tried to understand the concern that had fuelled his spanking. But despite the slightness of his frame, he had never truly felt the cold, not in a way that warranted fear. But children often can't imagine danger until they experience it for themselves.

With the spring sun came a pulling away of winter's chains. Oliver helped his uncle separate the last of the firewood that had still been in the yard when the snow had first arrived. Ice had bonded the junks together and anchored them to the earth. As the town was thawing, it became possible to get the axe between the pieces of wood and separate them. Oliver's hands were red and raw from the rough, icy bark. He'd spent many summers chopping wood, but his hands still failed to toughen up the way his aunt claimed they would.

Despite the rise and fall of the tide and the constant movement of ocean swell, the sheltered harbour of Salvage still turns to ice in cold winters. Storms break the surface and suck the ice out to sea, but the innermost shores and inlets stay caught, so the ice has a chance to grow solid. This year the ice had stretched well out into the bay. It had been thick enough that wharves were heaved up, and the cradles that supported them had been shattered. The bulk of work ahead of the townsfolk grew day by day. As snow and ice receded, the damages they'd done were revealed.

Oliver was looking out past the ice to the dark blue of the ocean. He could feel the slightest breeze coming off the waves and in over the small yard. It felt good, despite its chill. The screen door clapped closed behind him, and Oliver turned to see his aunt.

Elizabeth looked at the bare patch on the lawn where the wood had been heaved up and separated, and then she looked at the boy.

"Go on then. Get gone," she shouted with a wave of her hand.

Oliver's eyes widened and he didn't hesitate. He ran from the yard before the last syllable had left his aunt's tongue. He turned away from her as he ran, hoping she wouldn't see the smile spreading across his face and call him back, uncomfortable with being too kind. Oliver ran along the shoreline, his feet finding balance on the rocky edge, the ocean a short but steep drop below him. He followed the shore as it cut in and out, points and coves starting and ending without any pattern. Ice lined the rocky beach. In some places it was broken away, letting the salt water see the sun, but in others the ice held strong, still claiming to be a reinvention of the shoreline.

Oliver skipped and ran, relishing in his freedom. He followed the patches of exposed earth and rock where he could, but he didn't shy from trouncing through the snow when there was no path of clear ground. The air was just warm enough that there was no harm in how quickly his socks were getting wet.

The snow was plentiful between the rocks, filling the cracks and crevices and turning sharp cliffs to slopes. Anywhere that the earth offered shade, the ice held on, hiding from the sun for the last of its days. Oliver began running along the rocky outreach at the centre of Salvage Harbour. The long point separated the fish-plant cove and Bishop's Harbour. The rocks towered high at the centre: impossible to build upon, but perfect for a child to climb.

Oliver had created a game for himself. He weaved back and forth, up and down, following the exposed rocks. He made big standing jumps over patches of snow that were unavoidable and tiptoed along the narrow ridges of rocky peaks.

Oliver was contemplating his course, deciding which jump would give him the most options, when he heard the sound of running water coming from somewhere near him. Standing still, at the spot where the sound seemed the loudest, Oliver realized that it was coming from beneath the snow. Spring runoff was carving tunnels through the last remnants of winter. He looked around the harbour at the sheer rock that protected it, enclosed it. Wet with the spring, it looked softer than usual. As winter steadily receded, all the water from the clifftops made for the sea. Brooks and streams, with lifespans as short as the ice, weaved everywhere and in every direction, racing continuously downward.

When the water reached the sea, it disappeared under thick ice. The ocean had lifted the shelf of ice up off the pebbles, and there was enough space between ground and frozen sea water that the stream could join the bay unhindered. These were ballicatters, ice that formed great structures all along the shoreline, huge jagged chunks of solid sea heaved and reshaped over the course of the winter. While Oliver watched the water disappearing, he heard the distant sound of children. Voices, shouts and giggles were coming from just around the point. Oliver slowly made his way up along the point, which hid them from his view. He followed the streams of spring runoff and paused at a fork, trying to convince himself that he wasn't choosing his path exclusively for the sounds of other children's fun.

Oliver had learned from school, and summers around the harbour, that the other kids didn't usually play games he could join in. He wasn't sure how it had come to be that way, why he always seemed to find the kids only after there were too many. He just knew that whenever he'd asked, the teams were full or the game didn't require another player. Sometimes the other children ran away when he got close to them. When he was younger, he thought this was its own game, and he'd chase them as far as he could. But they always ended up hiding, or going into someone's house. Once, he'd caught up to one of the boys, Gary Matchim, but when Oliver had reached out and tagged him, Gary only looked back with a glare and continued running.

But Oliver would be eleven by the end of this spring and knew better than to think that chasing them was supposed to be fun for him. He didn't mind and found his own fun along the shorelines. He enjoyed the company of the ocean and some of the gulls that didn't cry too loud, and saw more when he was alone. Things wouldn't disappear because he wasn't speaking or laughing. Sometimes he did wish that he had someone to show his favourite places to. Or someone to talk to.

Oliver sat on the rocks at the top of the point and watched as the group of children began making their way out onto the ice.

The speed with which spring had arrived meant much of the ice was still thick, but the ocean had rolled underneath it enough times to break it apart. Now great pans of ice were loosely connected throughout the harbour. It was like the window of a mighty church. The panes were all of different sizes, and the lines between them were dark and distinct, but the stained glass of the sea was made up of only white and blue. The pans were slowly shifting apart. Over the next few days or weeks, depending on the weather, all the ice would break apart and melt, or it'd be pulled out to sea. But at that moment, the harbour was a mosaic of winter's end.

Some of the children had long sticks that they used as oars, pushing or sculling the pans of ice further into the harbour. Other children drove their sticks into the ocean floor and vaulted from one piece of ice to the next. They were all tentative at first, careful of the uneven footing of the ice and careful not to jump onto a pan that would tip them off into the knee-deep water or sink beneath their weight. Oliver watched as one of the youths made their way more than three pans from the shore. The ice was still sturdy, but the stakes were higher because the water beneath the children would be deeper with every jump they made. There were squeals of delight from those with less bravado than Rebecca, whose surname at that tender age was still Smith. Already ten feet from shore, she took a daring leap and landed herself in the middle of a narrow pan.

Courage was infectious. Invigorated by their companions' success, the children all began to move one pan and then another away from shore. Some of the children made a game of racing along the ice that encrusted the shoreline. They skipped and leapt parallel to the rocks, trying to see who could make their way across the most pans. Oliver watched this for a while. He looked back at Rebecca, who had stopped her outward journey some five pans from shore. To the left, starting from a different point, Johnathan Genge was beginning to match her progress.

Johnathan didn't hold a stick as he jumped. He leapt from one pan to the next with his arms at his sides, moving so casually that he could just as easily have been hopping his way down the road. Oliver marvelled at the power in his legs as they propelled him through the air with an easy grace. Johnathan was a year older, but he'd always been nice to Oliver. When Oliver asked to join the other children in their games, Johnathan was never one of the kids who shouted names at him. And only once had Johnathan been one of the children throwing snowballs at him on his walk home from school.

Johnathan wore only a t-shirt, trousers and his heavy rubber boots. The other children still wore their winter clothing, thick shirts and jackets, but Johnathan's exposed arms showed off his fortitude. Even though he was still just a boy, the tone in his arms was already noticeable to Oliver. His limbs were thicker and stronger than Oliver's little arms would ever be.

Brazenly, Johnathan jumped onto the very ice pan that Rebecca was steadying herself upon. The pan heaved up and down for a moment under the excessive weight. Before it had even levelled, Johnathan jumped onto another one. The children closer to the shore hollered and shouted at this, excited by Johnathan's reckless behaviour.

"Look at Gengy!" Clayton Saunders shouted. "Look at 'im!"

"That's nothing, sure," Gary, the Matchim boy, called back. He began taking his own leaps out onto the pans with clear intent to race Johnathan to the most distant pieces of ice.

Oliver felt excitement tightening his chest and rising in his throat. He could play this game. He didn't even need to be invited or ask. It was just the harbour and the ice. He could start from the point where he was sitting, far enough away from the others that they wouldn't need to shout at him, or tell him to go away. But if he made his way out, jumping between the pieces of ice on his own, he could end up just a few pans away from them, and it would almost be like they were all playing together.

Oliver clambered down over the rocks and jumped out onto the closest ice pan. He didn't take the time to search for a stick. He didn't need one: he could jump across the pans like Johnathan.

The first couple sheets of ice were easy. They were so thick and solid that jumping between them was no different from jumping between the rocks. In the shallows, the ice was floating just above the bottom, and the addition of Oliver's weight pushed the pan down against the pebbly ocean floor before it had a chance to tip. The third pan wobbled more with Oliver's weight. It was floating freely, and he had to still himself for a moment to keep it from tipping over.

Once he was balanced, he tiptoed towards the edge of the ice pan, just close enough that it wasn't dipping into the water under his weight, and then he jumped to the next pan. The landing on the next couple pans was easier. They were big sheets of ice, more than buoyant enough to support a couple children. He was making his way further and further out.

Gary Matchim was almost parallel to Oliver, but he'd chosen a thin piece of ice. Every time he shifted or stepped, the pan wobbled and made small splashes in the water. Gary let out a sudden shriek, his voice cracking at the loudest point, as his toes were dunked underwater.

The children all laughed at this, and Gary uttered a series of curse words that would have brought out his mother's largest wooden spoon. Finally succumbing to his poor decision, he made a clumsy jump back to his previous pan and fell onto his backside, but on a larger, stable piece of ice.

Oliver watched Gary's struggle, but it didn't deter him. He kept going. He made another jump, and then another. Although Oliver had made it further out than Rebecca, there was a jitter in his legs. His knees weren't knocking together, but his thighs had begun to quiver. Shore seemed like a long way off now. The pans shifted and turned on the ocean's surface. The sea between the ice was deep that far out. There was no bottom. The blue was so dark it resembled the night sky more than water.

A breeze came in off the ocean. It filled the undone jackets of the flipsying children and blew the hair out of their faces. The breeze was followed by the slightest wave. It wasn't a swell large enough to cause much disturbance, but Oliver could feel the water move through the pan beneath his feet.

Johnathan Genge's progress had slowed now. The further into the bay he worked, the greater the space between the pans. Johnathan's decision not to use a stick meant that all he could do was leap from one pan to the next and wait for another to drift closer. He rocked his hips, trying to transfer some momentum to the ice, but this accomplished nothing. Some of the ice—even as far out as he was—remained thick, wide and strong. On these stable pieces, Johnathan stooped over with hands on his knees, taking deep breaths as he plotted a safe route from one big pan to the next.

Oliver's movements were still continuous, but they weren't direct; he was cutting back and forth across the field of ice as he progressed further out into the bay. Although there was now a wide gap between Oliver and most of the other children who had ventured out onto the ice, the space between him and Johnathan was steadily decreasing. Oliver willed Johnathan to turn around, to see how well he was doing. Oliver wanted Johnathan to look back and see that he had come just as far. He wanted him to see that he was brave, that he was his competition. Oliver wanted Johnathan to see that they were equals.

Despite all the bravery that Oliver wanted to be noticed, the ice pan beneath him shivered and shook. Oliver's quivering legs were transferring their vibration to the ice, and tiny ripples were emanating from its every edge. He bit his lip as he looked at the space between himself and the next pan. It would be a leap over a large stretch of ocean.

The sea breeze came again. It blew harder across his cheeks and Oliver gulped it in, willing the chilled and salty air to fill his lungs. The familiar smell of the ocean calmed him, despite the cold that it carried. He swallowed. Willing his legs to move, Oliver jumped with one foot stretched out in front of him. The distance was greater than the stretch of his legs, but his footing had been sure, and the jump had been confident. He cleared the gap but landed needing to slow himself with two stuttering steps. He stopped just short of the edge of the new pan. There was a murmur of excitement from the children far back on the shore.

Johnathan was only a couple pans ahead of Oliver. He was stationary, rocking slightly back and forth as if hoping to coax his pan closer to another.

Another breeze came, stronger than before. The two boys had to bend their knees as a wave rolled the ice beneath their feet. Shouts came from behind them as the swell shook the pans closer to shore.

The wave wasn't alone. It was followed by two more, each smaller than its predecessor. The roll of the sea was gentle, rhythmic—but the boys still had to watch the water, constantly ready to change their footing and redistribute their weight. This time, when the sea air filled Oliver's jacket and ignited goosebumps on Johnathan's forearms, it couldn't be called a breeze. The air—a cold that almost stung—whipped across their cheeks. A northerly gust. The winds were coming up.

Johnathan's legs were shaking just as Oliver's had been. He turned around and looked back towards the other children and the shore. Oliver saw that his face was white and his lips were tight. Johnathan's deep well of adolescent courage was finally beginning to run dry. When Johnathan saw Oliver so close by, he smiled at him. Perhaps it was a smile to cover up his fear. Perhaps it was encouragement for the competition to continue. Or perhaps it was a smile of affection for his pan-hopping companion. Oliver didn't care what made Johnathan smile at him; he just grinned back, brighter and bigger than he'd ever smiled before.

The boys were keenly aware of the growing winds and knew that their distance from shore made them more vulnerable to the ocean's weather. They didn't know that the tide was making its way out, pulling the pans with it. Since the motion of the tide matched the direction they were leaping, they hadn't noticed the ocean assisting their progress. Just as they hadn't noticed the pans being shifted closer behind them, bottlenecked by the mouth of the cove, but drifting further apart as the bay opened in to the ocean.

Johnathan held Oliver's eyes, grinning. He opened his mouth, perhaps about to suggest a truce, a return to shore. Or maybe quite the opposite. As the two boys looked at one another, the ocean rose up and rolled its way into the harbour.

Johnathan's smile disappeared as the front of his ice pan lifted. He hadn't been watching the water. He wasn't prepared. His weight was too far to one side of the ice, and he didn't bend his knees in time to stabilize himself. In a motion quicker than any of the children watching were prepared for, the ice pan flipped.

Johnathan was thrown backward. His head collided with the thick ice of a pan behind him, and his whole body was dunked under the surface. His heavy rubber boots quickly filled with the sub-zero ocean waters.

There were squeals and shouts from shore, but most of the children made no sound. They watched the water, holding a collective breath.

Oliver was focussed on the place that Johnathan had disappeared. His body balanced itself intuitively, absorbing the rise and fall of his pan as the ocean rushed the shore. Behind him, the boys and girls dropped to their hands and knees, bracing for the coming wave.

All the children waited for Johnathan to come to the surface, but the ocean had smoothed itself. There wasn't a ripple, not a singular blemish to prove that, a moment ago, the water had swallowed a young boy whole.

What happened next is a matter of quite some debate.

What's certain is that after only a couple moments of waiting, Oliver Brown went into the water as well.

Clayton Saunders claimed loudly that Oliver had fallen in a manner not dissimilar to Johnathan. But Clayton had barely left the shore. Rebecca and Gary—and any other children who had ventured further out into the bay—said with absolute confidence that Oliver Brown had dived into the ocean on purpose.

The children watched, now waiting for not just one head to appear, but two. Shouts began to come from the group, from all of them and none of them at once. The children called to the boys again and again, so loud and so quick that none of them really knew who was calling what.

Rosie Ryan, one of the youngest kids, had the sense to do more than yell at the ocean's surface. She raced down the shore, tears streaming down her face, shouting that two of the boys had fallen into the water.

Barry and Clyde Newport were in the midst of repairing their ice-heaved wharf when they saw Rosie running down the shore, screaming at a pitch and volume that turned heads and raised hairs. They stilled their hammers and looked on in confusion for a moment. Their tools fell to the rocks when they made sense of her words, when they realized she was yelling about icy deaths.

Word spread like oil on water. Clyde's wife heard the shouting and ran to the next house. She told Franny Newport, who told Dorman, who shouted to Stella and the three Felthams all at once. No one stopped to ask who had fallen in. Names and blood relation didn't matter: someone from their town was in trouble, and so all together—all at once—the village responded.

Those who hadn't heard the yelling were now beginning to see the commotion through their windows. Adults sprinted along the shore faster than their legs had carried them in years. A punt was heaved onto the backs of three men—a feat that should have taken five—and was run to the water's edge.

Barry Newport shouted at the children when he got to the shore. "Where'd they go under?" He had run into the water and was already run knee deep. He was focussed on doing as much as he could and didn't consider the cold.

The children all yelled and shouted, pointing to the place the two boys were last seen.

"How long ago?" Barry said.

Clayton's face was wet with tears. "They're gone. They're gone. It's been ten minutes. It's been ages."

"No! They only just went under," Rebecca screeched, still

standing on an offshore pan.

Barry shouted at her. "Git in from there!"

"Gone forever!" Clayton screeched.

The punt had reached the shore. Its belly was laid on the ice pans, waiting to make it to open water. Three men were on either side now, but as they tried to push it out, the ice gave way beneath their feet. The outflowing tide was pulling the ice just as quickly as the men could drag the boat across it. The pans refused to be pushed apart to let the boat float upon the water.

More adults arrived at the beach. The punt was frantically pushed further out. Someone heaved an axe into the ice, trying to separate it and make space for the boat to push through.

No one spoke as they worked—but in the heads of every fisherman, a clock was ticking.

They couldn't know how long it had been. Knowing wouldn't change their actions; they were already doing everything they could. They knew how long they'd been trying, though. They were all too aware of the seconds becoming minutes, and the minutes compiling, one by one, shortening the rope of an anchor still falling towards the bottom.

But no one stopped. No one stopped trying.

The youngest children on shore were scooped up and taken away, removed from the scene before they saw something they wouldn't be able to forget. A dory left from the other side of the cove. It was further away from the place the boys went under, but as no ice was against the shore, the men hoped they'd have a clearer, shorter path across the bay.

A scanning and a counting of the children had revealed who was missing. Johnathan Genge's mother, Mary, stood on shore with a hand at her throat. She was too scared to cry, too shocked to scream.

Their eyes on the water. The townspeople were desperately hoping for something to appear that wasn't white or dark blue, for any sign of the kids, anything that wasn't spring sea.

Rebecca, who still hadn't entirely come in off the ice, shouted something indecipherable and pointed to a place at the edge of the solid shore ice some hundred yards further out in the cove than where the boys had gone under.

Dark hair, matted to a tiny head, bobbed up and down between the solid ice and floating pans. The adults all began racing towards it. The dory was left behind, still only partially in the water. As the rescuers ran, some across the pans, some along the shore, some already waist deep in the frigid waters, they saw Oliver Brown pull his whole body up onto the ice. They all watched in confusion as he turned around and reached back into the water. His legs were extended behind him as he first put his arms, then his head, then his entire upper body—right to his waist—back under the water. Oliver began bending his knees and trying to crawl backward along the ice.

Clyde Newport was the first to reach him. He grabbed the boy's belt and pulled up hard. He heaved the child backward. The soaked clothing of the boy made him weigh twice as much as he should have. Barry joined Clyde. His hands clutched Oliver's shirt, and they pulled him out of the water. When his head was back above the surface, and then his arms, the men were shocked to see Oliver's slight hands clutching with white knuckles to the shirt of Johnathan Genge.

Both of the boys were pulled from the water as more and more adults were reaching the edge of the ice. Johnathan's father, Clarke, reached the boys with a face as white as the ice. Oliver held tight to Johnathan as they were dragged back along the ice, closer to safety. Johnathan's body was completely motionless.

Murmuring, "Is he going to be okay? Is he going to be okay?" Oliver was pulled away from his companion. No one offered him a response. Again and again the words spilled out of him, asking with such insistence that it seemed he'd have repeated them for the rest of his life until he was answered.

But no one had an answer to give him.

Clyde Newport was pressing on Johnathan's chest. First with open hand, and then in desperation with closed fist, hammering the youth's body, trying to knock the water out of his lungs. Clarke Genge stood over Clyde with a hand on the man's back. His eyes were wet and full, and his every muscle was tense, but he could do no more than what was being done. Clyde put his mouth against the child's and breathed out hard, hoping to force air into him. Johnathan's face was ice cold, but the North Atlantic in April can suck away heat in a single moment. Blue lips weren't enough to make Clyde give up.

There was nothing to be done in that moment but watch. Barry held his breath as his brother tried to breathe life into the boy. And only then, Barry would come to claim, did he notice Oliver's continuous stream of questioning. Barry would say that he turned to the boy and that he didn't seem to be the slightest bit out of breath. Barry would avow that, even as a droplet of ice water fell from Oliver's nose, the child never shivered and his cheeks remained flushed. He looked perfectly healthy, while his companion looked as if the water had sucked the very soul out of his body.

Aubrey reached the group gathered on the ice. He whipped his jacket off his back and wrapped it around his great-nephew.

"I don't know, son. I don't know," he said, finally giving Oliver an answer.

Oliver looked up at his uncle, warm tears replacing the cold wetness on his cheeks.

"I tried," he said. "I tried my hardest. I tried my hardest. I really did. I tried my hardest."

Aubrey squeezed him tight.

Then, in a moment that is collectively agreed upon to have been nothing short of a miracle, Johnathan Genge began to cough.

Mary Genge was already calling from the shore when the men began racing back in off the ice. The danger hadn't passed yet. Two children were sent to the Genges' saltbox with instruction to stoke the fire—stoke it as much as they could— and once it was burning hot, put the kettle and every pot in the house on top of it.

Johnathan's wet clothing was torn off him as they moved. The adults offered what dry articles they had to keep him covered on the way back to the house. The boy's skin was as white as the ice; he looked almost as cold as he felt in his father's arms. The whole town watched as he was held with hope and raced to shore with fear. Silently, they prayed for the boy to fight off the cold—for his breathing to not grow any more shallow.

Almost every eye was on Johnathan as he fought for his life. But two boys were being carried to shore. The problem was that, by all accounts, the other boy was just fine. Oliver could have walked to shore himself, they would say. He could have swum, they'd come to say. It went unmentioned in the moment; it went unnoticed by many. But when the urgency of the event came to pass, exactly how fine Oliver Brown had been that day became a story often repeated in a whisper.

Aubrey would say that his great-nephew had come up for air. That neither of the boys had been in for nearly as long as people thought. Aubrey would say that things seemed to happen slowly in the panic, and really it had just been a minute or two. Not the ten, fifteen, twenty that people came to claim. Aubrey would say that nothing was peculiar about it. The boys had gotten lucky. And that might be what actually happened. But that doesn't mean it's what the people of Salvage would choose to believe.

Aubrey might have been speaking the truth of the matter, but that doesn't mean he believed it himself.

Tibb's Eve

The evening before a day that will never come. Celebrated in many parts of Newfoundland on the twenty-third of December.

A teenaged Oliver Brown finished fastening the buttons of his coat as he left the steps of his aunt and uncle's house, but his fingers didn't leave the top button. Before he walked off the lawn that was hidden beneath a few inches of powdery snow, he began undoing his jacket again. The air was cool, but not as cool as other Christmases he remembered. Less snow had fallen than he hoped for by the end of December, but even a mild December night was better than the stifling warmth of the house. He willed for his open coat to billow with an ocean breeze, but there was too much stillness in the night. He walked with determined intention, unique to a person with nowhere in particular to go, away from where he had been.

The cold was more familiar to him than the damp heat of too many bodies converging around a table too small. The convergence reminded Oliver of the night over six years before, when friends and family had waited with bated breath for the return of Bobby Ryan. The cold was more comforting than all those bodies that wished he wasn't amongst them.

Since childhood, Oliver had been taught that some parts of his nature should be kept to himself. He had done up his coat as he left his aunt Elizabeth and uncle Aubrey's house, knowing he'd be followed by declarations of irresponsibility if he didn't do so. He had come to learn that his own indifference to the temperature outside would only raise questions amongst his aunt and uncle's guests, the kinds of questions that other young people his age could brush off. But the people of Salvage didn't regard him quite the same way that they did anyone else. As much as they might have pretended they did.

Oliver let his coat whip behind him as he made a confident jump from the roadside to the beach rocks that the road followed. He looked forward as he moved, absent of concern for the terrain beneath his feet. His eyes were on a harbour mouth only faintly visible through gentle starlight but distinguishable through familiarity.

Time doesn't change the line of the coast. The shores will be manipulated, they will be pummeled and they will recede. They will be washed with forgotten and foreign debris. Structures will rise and be allowed to fall again; they will host fires and floods without discrimination. But the boundary between sea and land that constituted the first maps and charts are influenced only by things that take longer than any human lifetime. The coastline remains, and coves and inlets change but never move. Rocky points have a permanency so dependable that Oliver no longer needed to see the ground before him to be able to follow the crests and dips that allowed a path along the rocks out into the harbour.

The early darkness of winter evenings had fallen on Salvage. A new moon had encouraged a sticky kind of black to envelope the town, but it was December twenty-third and there was an exceptional addition of man-made light in the harbour town. Windows were ablaze with candles that would normally have been douted hours before. The tips of the A-frames were adorned with stars composed of leftover light bulbs, and more than one bonfire burned bright along the beaches.

Oliver made his way to the tip of an all too familiar point. The same point he'd once ventured out from when trying to join the other children flipsying. The same point that he had walked a hundred times since and that the residents of Salvage had come to associate with his silhouette.

By now, in the latter part of his fifteenth year, Oliver's form was synonymous with the horizon. His figure was commonplace on the outcrops and clifftops. The folks of the town had already begun whispering that Oliver possessed a different means of moving. They'd say that the rocks were bare and then he stood upon them, with no space between the two moments. They'd say that he stood impossibly still for hours. What they meant, of course, was that they didn't look long enough to see him arrive, nor to see him go again. But he was old enough, his habits consistent enough, his lineage murky enough, that no one bothered to offer him the benefit of the doubt.

Oliver could feel the sharp edges of the rocks through the thin soles of his boots. He took a meandering path to the outer edge of the point, following the only course that the rocks allowed. A part of him he couldn't ignore knew that the water offered a more direct route to his destination, but reservations his upbringing had instilled in him ensured that he kept to dry land.

As he got further away from his aunt and uncle's house, he further undid his clothing, knowing the night was too dark for anyone to see his shirt unbuttoned. Oliver's stomach was twisted and aching in a manner he couldn't justify. It felt like he hadn't eaten in far too long. It felt like he'd never be hungry again. He wanted to be sick, but his throat was too tight to allow anything to come back up.

He found a familiar position on the furthest rocks. Winter had arrived but it hadn't settled. The snow on the ground was still fresh, and the salt water in the bay still rose and fell against the rocks. The water was so cold it seemed thick. The waves only lapped and never crashed, as if afraid that moving too much would risk freezing, risk changing form.

Oliver found his breathing and tried to match it to the quiet motion of the water, willing his heart to mimic the sea's rhythm just as he had as a child. But he couldn't find the beat; he was too distracted.

~

Hours before, he had looked out the kitchen window towards the point on which he now stood, willing his mind to be in a place his body wasn't. But now, sitting upon the rocks, he couldn't pull his mind from the perspective of that kitchen table.

His uncle had cut a cookie in half to share with him. A rich ball of butter cocoa and dried coconut. It was a treat intended for Christmas Day, but there was a small allowance for a taste of it to be stolen a couple days early. Aunt Elizabeth had pretended not to notice when Aubrey pulled the cookie from the hidden tin, but she let out an audible huff when he cut it down the middle and offered Oliver a piece.

Oliver finished the cookie while he sipped his tea. The foreign taste of coconut was rich and tangy on his tongue. He wasn't sure about the flavour, but it was better than the taste of Tetley. He'd come to prefer more evaporated milk than water in his tea, growing less and less fond of tea as he got older.

There was a knock, quick and sharp, and the porch door was thrown open. Their neighbour Missy Smith walked in without waiting for an invitation. She was looking down as she entered.

"Irene and May will be over now the once," she said, kicking sticky snow from her boots, more concerned with the mess she was making on the linoleum floor than with the recognition of her arrival. "They're over to Colin and Sandy's, and you knows what it's like trying to drag them outta there."

Without instruction or suggestion, Aubrey rose from his seat at the end of the table. Oliver began to stand as well. But as he did, Aubrey laid a hand upon his shoulder. The gesture was passive, but his hand was heavy, holding the boy in his seat. Albert shifted to the inside of the table, taking a seat next to Oliver and freeing up a seat next to Aunt Elizabeth for Missy.

Visitors are to be expected on the twenty-third of December. The entire harbour seemed to share in a succumbing to temptation. The special items intended to be enjoyed on Christmas Day would be sampled just a couple days early every year. It became a common practice—a tradition—to visit neighbours along the shore and experience what indulgences they had reserved for the occasion.

Satisfied with the dryness of her boots, Missy hung her coat on the rack by the door and made her way into the kitchen. Elizabeth got up, clearing away Oliver's and Aubrey's dessert plates, and Missy took Elizabeth's seat, ignoring the empty chair that Aubrey had left for her and positioning herself as far from Oliver as the table allowed.

"My dear, I tell ya," Missy said, "we started off over to Barry and Franny Newports'. And I mean, they were hospitable enough, but it's cold enough to skin ya in there. Ya knows what they're like. Won't put a split in the stove till ya can't feel yer fingers."

"I know, maid, and even then they'd sooner offer you mitts," Elizabeth said.

"Yuh. Not fit. I was there long enough, had a cup o' tea, but sure me teeth were clatterin' by the time Irene and Art said they were leavin'. So I carried on with them then."

"And you went over to Colin and Sandy's then?" Elizabeth asked from the sink. She had cleaned and put away every dish in the place, but now she scrubbed the sink itself for the second time that day, in preparation of more guests arriving.

"No," Missy said. "Art's got the thirst in 'em there tonight, so we went straight over to the Genges."

Oliver's ears perked up a little at that family name. He listened to Missy a little more intently.

"Mary was only just cleanin' up for dinner, hadn't even had their tea yet—you knows they always eats some late—and Clarke was down to the beach, throwin' some old traps on a bonfire that Johnathan's got goin'."

Oliver looked out the small kitchen window to the water. He couldn't see any fire burning from where he sat, but they would have been in the next cove over, rocks and houses hiding them from view.

"So we had to stay then 'till Clarke got back, and sure not a minute after he was through the door, Mary took out that ol' accordion." Missy punctuated her sentence with a sharp tut. Sucking air through her tongue against the top of her mouth.

"Oh my souls," Elizabeth said, shaking her head and returning to the table herself. Elizabeth also refused to take the place that Aubrey had left. Instead, she shuffled behind Missy to sit at the far end of the table.

"I know, my dear. I know," Missy continued. "So I just couldn't be at it. I went straight back out the door and up to Colin and Sandy's."

"I don't blame ya one bit," Elizabeth said.

While the women continued to chat, Aubrey took Oliver's teacup from in front of him. It was still half full, but the tea had gone cold. Aubrey walked into the kitchen with both cups, emptying them into the perfectly cleaned sink.

Elizabeth didn't even look towards her husband. While she wouldn't normally stand for him doing dishes, she knew better than to think that's what he was up to. There was a clinking of glass bottles as Aubrey rummaged beneath the sink before coming back to the table.

To Oliver's surprise, Aubrey laid a teacup in front of him again, the bottom of the cup filled with a dark liquid. Oliver looked from the drink to his uncle, but his uncle didn't look back, pretending to be unaware of what he had done.

"Yes, so, as I was sayin', I went over to Colin and Sandy's. Now, they must have had some good year." Missy raised her eyebrows high and nodded towards Elizabeth.

"That right?"

"Sure. We had to take off our boots when we got there. Tore up all the floors in the house, and they got carpet laid in there now."

"Yes, sure I heard that," Elizabeth said, not wanting to seem out of the loop.

"Yuh, whole house done in it. Must be nice."

"Must be nice."

"Now I don't mean nothin' by that. Colin works hard."

"Oh yes, I knows, maid. But ya know, not havin' nar youngster around makes a penny go further." Elizabeth threw a sideways glance at Oliver.

Oliver was focussed on the black liquid in his mug. It smelled of sweet spruce trees. He brought the callibogus to his lips, and the first swallow almost made him choke. The drink of rum, molasses and spruce beer wasn't as strong as the dark rum his uncle would drink, but it still burned hot in his unaccustomed mouth.

Oliver's spluttering brought a muffled chuckle from his uncle and drew the eyes of his aunt. She opened her mouth, perhaps about to reprimand Oliver, or his uncle, or the pair of them. But then the kitchen door swung open once more.

Irene and May came through the door in the midst of giggles.

"Happy Christmas!" Irene called, cheeks already rosy from the evening's indulgences.

"Happy Christmas," Elizabeth said, getting up once more, this time to collect refreshments for the new arrivals. She was in a constant state of standing up and then sitting down only to get back up again.

"My goodness, Liza, you should see the carpet that Sandy's got down there," May called from the doorway, unwrapping a scarf from around her neck.

"See, I told ya," Missy said.

"Art will be over now the once. Hopefully before he's in too much of a state." Irene emphasized the *too*, accepting that her husband would be far less than sober by the time he rejoined her.

The two women sat at the table, filling the last two empty seats. They repositioned their bodies to face Missy and Elizabeth, away from Aubrey and Oliver. Elizabeth placed a teapot in the centre of the table, laid atop a folded dish towel to save the wood. Next to the teapot she placed a tall brown bottle with a cork that snapped into place. The physical presence of the two vessels of liquid implied options, suggesting that there would be a choice for the guests. But as Oliver watched, Elizabeth wordlessly picked up the brown bottle and poured it into all four women's cups. Missy put up a fake protest as the bottle hovered over hers.

"Oh no, I couldn't sure," she said.

Elizabeth snorted and poured anyway.

"Oh not too much. You knows I don't drink, Liza."

"Oh yes, and I suppose you weren't havin' neither drink back at Sandy's," May said.

"And you didn't have a tipple into the Newports'," Irene added.

"Well . . ." Missy said, "I s'pose I can have a nip."

Elizabeth had filled their glasses with squatum. She'd made it with the last of the summer's partridgeberries and let it ferment in the cellar, getting sweeter and boozier as it waited for Christmas.

May had a parcel tucked under her arm. It was wrapped in wrinkled red tissue paper that had likely been dyed with the same berries that the women now drank. She laid the parcel on the table. Oliver could see the gentle rips at the paper's edge, the old creases where it had been folded to wrap a different gift in a different year before being ironed out for reuse.

"You wouldn't believe it, but I ran into your sister on the way out the door over at Colin and Sandy's. She wanted me to give that to you," May said. "Said to say happy Christmas to you and Aub."

Elizabeth shook her head and sighed as she pulled the small parcel towards herself. "Sure Margret knows I'll see her in church two days from now."

"Ya know what she gets on like though," May tutted. "'Who's to say I'll make it till then.'"

"Oh my, not dramatic, knows," Elizabeth said.

"Margret's just bitter that you're not havin' her over for Christmas dinner," Irene said.

"I'd have her down if she'd come down, but you know she

wouldn't step foot in here."

"I know, I know," Irene said.

"Only so many times I'm going to hear her say 'no' before I stop asking." Elizabeth stared at the present on the table as if unable to touch it until grievances had been aired.

"I knows, foolish it is," Irene said "But that's what she's like."

"She won't change," May added.

"No point hoping that she will." Elizabeth finally pulled at the small piece of tape on the parcel. She gingerly tried to lift it from the tissue paper to keep the wrapping from being torn. Once she had unwrapped the gift, she folded up the paper once more, placing the fragile red rectangle at the corner of the table.

A piece of twine held together a pair of mittens, made of a silver-grey fur with speckles of black. As soon as they were revealed, Oliver was captured by the sight. Everyone at the table was taken aback for a moment. It was a more extravagant gift than they'd suspected.

"Oh my Lord," Missy said. "They're gorgeous, sure."

Elizabeth turned the mittens over in her hand. "Oh my, now why'd she go and do that."

Oliver found the gift just as enchanting as the adults around him. He stared at the soft, silky sheen of the fur. He couldn't place what it was. But he found it beautiful.

"One of the Felthams struck the creature with his punt. Few weeks back there now," May said. "Apparently, the prop chewed the skin up too bad to be used for much. But he figured Margret could make a few bits with it."

"Well, that's some nice of him too then," Elizabeth said. She rubbed her thumb back and forth across the wrist of the mitten, where a leather string was looped through at perfectly even intervals.

"Let us see then," Missy said, reaching for the mittens. She put one on her hand right away and then rubbed the supple material with her other hand. "They'll be some nice and warm."

"They look warm," Irene added.

Missy passed one of the mittens to Irene.

"Not much use, though. Too nice to wear anywhere, sure," Irene said, crossing her arms.

"Go on! Sure, they're meant to be worn," May said.

Irene passed a mitten to May. Missy took off the one she wore and handed it to Aubrey.

"Nice to wear to church," Aubrey said, passively looking at the mitten before handing it back to Elizabeth.

May handed the other mitten to Oliver then. He looked at it with wide eyes; there was something about it he found striking. The fur was coarse and soft all at once. The feeling of it on his fingers made him picture water beading off it.

"What is it?" Oliver asked, not looking up from the mitten.

Elizabeth cleared her throat loudly.

"Oh," May said.

Aubrey gently pulled the mitten from Oliver's hands and handed it back to Elizabeth. "I'd say a tanner, maybe a touch older," he said.

May began, "Perhaps I shouldn't have—"

"Well, there was certainly no need of her offering me such generosity," Elizabeth said. She placed the folded red wrapping paper over top of the mittens. She cleared her throat again and looked towards the door, as if expecting it to open.

May said, "I'm sure Margret didn't mean anything . . ." She glanced at the red wrapping paper and then at Oliver. She didn't look at his face, just at the table in front of him.

Oliver glanced at his tea mug and suddenly feared that he was going to be reprimanded for drinking the callibogus that his uncle Aubrey had poured.

A silence that Oliver didn't understand or recognize came over the room. His uncle Aubrey wasn't one to speak much, but Oliver wasn't accustomed to these women being silent. Rarely was there a silence when there were two of them; it seemed unfathomable that all four women had nothing to say. He looked around the table. All the adults seemed to be avoiding looking at each other. Oliver suddenly felt like a child again, excluded from the people he shared the room with, surrounded by that which he did not understand.

The door opened as it was knocked upon, again. The guests that Elizabeth had expected arrived and broke the muteness of the room.

"Happy Christmas!" Arthur came through the door without any of the same consideration for the state of his boots that Missy had offered. He seemed top heavy, stepping quickly forward as he came in, to catch himself.

"Happy Christmas," the table echoed back all at once, relieved to have been given something to say.

Elizabeth leered at Oliver, then she jerked her head up and her chin over her shoulder, demanding that he get out of his seat to make space for a guest.

"Leave him be, Liza." Aubrey spoke before Oliver had a chance to move. "I'll get a chair from the front porch."

Elizabeth didn't respond. She just stared at him as he stood and walked away.

Before Aubrey had a chance to cross the kitchen, however, the door opened again. "Merry Christmas," said Colin as he entered.

"Oh, merry Christmas, Colin!" Elizabeth said. "Nice of you to drop down."

"Nice of you to have me!" Colin said.

Elizabeth levelled her gaze on Oliver, and the boy stood without hesitation.

"Is Sandy coming down as well?" May asked.

"Oh, she might now the once. She just wanted to give the house a little clean before she came down."

"Vacuum that fancy carpet," Arthur said with a laugh. He already had a mug in his hand. Oliver hadn't even noticed a drink being produced. Irene glared at Arthur, but Colin seemed to find amusement in the comment and joined Arthur's laugh.

Oliver didn't particularly know Colin. He knew his name and face and had seen him around the town more than enough. But he'd never had a conversation with Colin, which made it particularly surprising to Oliver when the man spoke to him as he walked by.

"Sorry for taking your seat, lad," Colin said. "I don't mind standing," he added.

Oliver could feel his aunt opening her mouth to protest without needing to turn and look at her.

"That's okay." Oliver did his best to offer a smile that was polite and not just shocked.

Aubrey returned with the additional chair, and before he could even put it to the table, Arthur fell into it, a broad grin on his face.

While Colin and Aubrey were taking their seats, Arthur said, "Liza! Those are some nice mitts!" He reached for them before Elizabeth could pull them away. "Look at that, Irene. Some gorgeous sealskin mittens, wha'?"

Oliver felt something run up and down his spine. From his tailbone to his ears and back again, there was the slightest shiver, as if someone was tracing the bumps of his bones with a gentle touch. The silence that had been in the room before the men had arrived now returned, but this time, Oliver was beginning to understand it. He wasn't familiar with the term *tanner*. He had heard it before but didn't recognize it for what it was: a young seal.

"Yes, Art, I already looked at them." Irene spoke with a harsh tone at a low volume.

Arthur himself seemed to be flushed in the silence, but it was hard to tell if it was tied to anything other than alcohol.

Oliver became acutely aware of the fact that he was the only one in the room left standing. The difference between him and the others—a difference he could hardly understand—was given a physical place in that moment.

Aubrey grumbled something Oliver couldn't hear and began pouring drinks for the new arrivals. Within a few moments, the conversation had turned back to normal.

The adults talked amongst themselves, seemingly scarcely aware of Oliver. The tension of their silence passed without being addressed or explained. Oliver didn't understand exactly what it was about the sealskin mittens that had bothered everyone. He knew only the feeling that had filled him.

~

The walk out onto the harbour rocks had done little to calm the spinning of Oliver's mind and the turning of his stomach. But he gave up on finding the reason that he felt the way he did, and he slowly stopped himself from reliving the evening in the kitchen. No wind had willed itself to life across the water; there was still no gust to fill his undone shirt and jacket. But the slow lapping of the waves calmed his mind. And when he'd finally come to stop thinking about the mittens made of skin and what no one had said, his heart rate slowed to the rhythm of calm seas.

Token

A strange occurrence, usually inexplicable or supernatural, seen or heard before a death or serious disaster.

Two years before that day on the ice pans, nine-year-old Oliver had been sent in from chopping wood as a storm brewed. He kept his head down, staring at the white rings of past mugs on the bare table in front of him. He slowly opened and closed his hands, trying to work out the stiffness and push away the pain of the blisters. He appreciated that Uncle Aubrey had let him come in for an early tea, but now, alone in the house with Aunt Elizabeth, he was uncomfortable with being the subject of his uncle's command. His aunt didn't say anything to him, but her hands were heavy as she moved behind him. She dropped the kettle unceremoniously onto the stove, and clattered the cups and pans. The meal would be absent of care. Oliver willed for his uncle to come back in before Aunt Elizabeth decided to take out her frustrations on him.

She plopped a plate onto the table. Oliver stole a glance at her, but she wasn't looking back at him. She didn't have the flush of anger on her face that Oliver had expected. Her eyes were on the small window over the kitchen sink, but she was looking well past the harbour, out to the same place that Aubrey had been trying to find.

There was no cutlery: the plate held toutons and a large dollop of molasses. Oliver reached for one of the pieces of fried dough, burned black in some places, soft and puffy in others. Oliver's mouth watered with the smell of the scrunchins, the fried salt pork that was stuck to the toutons.

His mouth was open and ready when Elizabeth suddenly said, "You best be giving thanks for that feed, Oliver Brown. I'm not raising a heathen. Yer bad enough as it is."

Oliver closed his mouth and hung his head a little lower. He placed the touton back on the plate and put his hands together. He closed his eyes and quickly murmured a thank you, knowing the words of grace but not yet the meaning. Opening his eyes, he licked his lips and dragged the touton through the black, sticky molasses and jammed as much of it into his mouth as he could manage.

Elizabeth laid a cup of tea, white and thick from canned milk, in front of Oliver. Her movements were gentler than before. She moved back to the kitchen; he heard the glug from the jug of fresh water as the kettle was refilled.

"The fish is fair off Little Denier," Elizabeth said. "There wasn't any need of going out that far."

Oliver tried to keep his lips from smacking, not wanting to make a sound and interrupt her. She wasn't speaking to him, but she wasn't not speaking to him either.

"Greed," she said, with a clicking of her tongue. "There's a fifth thing that'll never say 'enough': young fishermen. And you don't get to be an old fisherman if you don't learn to be satisfied."

Oliver mopped up the last of the molasses on his plate with the smallest corner of a touton. Fingers sticky enough that they could hardly be pulled apart.

"Gluttony." She dropped a wet cloth in front of him and took away his empty plate. "It seems like a simple sin until a nor'easter comes from nowhere."

Oliver wiped his hands and face with the damp cloth. He was thorough, not wanting his aunt to scrub his skin. He picked up his tea and drank in deep gulps.

"Gluttony has got no place on the water—"

"And gluttony has got nothing to do with it." Aubrey's voice was low enough to resonate, but his words were sharp as he walked into the room. "Bobby's got seven mouths to feed up on the hill and an eighth on the way. Gluttony is when not enough is left for the needy. Not when those in need try to get enough."

"There's no need of them testing the ocean like that, Aub. You've been doing fine off Little Denier, no need."

"No. Elizabeth, I won't have any of that." He sat down heavy at the end of the kitchen table. "It was a fine day this morning. The risk was reasonable. Don't blame those men for the seas turning."

"I'm not blaming 'em."

"No, but yer damning them before you've started praying for 'em. And with May about to come through the door."

Elizabeth huffed.

"And with Bobby's brother coming up the shore."

Oliver's plate was dropped into the kitchen sink with a clatter.

"Aubrey . . ."

Aubrey held his hand up, but he kept his head down. There was resignation, not fierceness, in his expression.

"It's his brother, Liza. I won't have him sitting alone, all the way down there on the beach, waiting to see if the water will forgive," he said.

Elizabeth sighed again, deeper and longer this time, wanting Aubrey to hear it from start to finish. She added more water to the kettle, and then she reached below the kitchen sink and pulled out a bottle of rum. She placed the bottle in the centre of the table and waved at Oliver, shooing him from his seat.

The weather brought the night with it. Clouds, heavy and dark, came in quickly with the wind. The sky seemed to be growing thicker, denser—texture added with every gust. The wind had stopped blowing now and had turned instead to whipping and pounding. Clapboard and thin walls kept the rain and gusts out, but Elizabeth kept looking to the kettle. Imperceivable breaks in the house's insulation created a constant whistle indoors, as if the weather itself was reaching boiling point.

It was dark when May finally arrived, despite the sun not being due to set for another couple hours. She was tight lipped and stern faced, not yet upset enough for it to show in her features. May's sister, Irene, came not long after, knocking on the door with a gentle rhythm that at first couldn't be deciphered from the rattling of the wind. Irene looked more concerned than May. Her face was pale, her slight fingers clutching at the buttons of her jacket. She looked like she'd seen the ghosts of men not yet dead. Irene's husband, Arthur, appeared within the hour, after he'd stoked the fire at home and made sure the windows were closed up. Irene and Arthur's oldest daughter was left at home to take care of her younger siblings as well as her cousins.

May and Bobby's children hadn't been given an explanation as to where their father was, or why they would be spending the night with their cousins. Arthur usually fished with Bobby, but he'd stayed ashore that day. The nets needed needle work and his hands were steadiest. Even Oliver, despite his youth, could tell that Arthur had a storm of his own behind his eyes.

The adults took positions around the kitchen table. Aubrey sat quietly at one end, Elizabeth on the other. She was often up and down, retrieving fixings for the guests from the kitchen cupboards. Oliver sat on his cot in the corner of the living room, as far away from the adults as the small home allowed. May had looked towards him briefly when she'd walked into the room, but her eyes had hesitated on his face no longer than they did on the rocking chair in the other corner. They all spoke openly, as if the kitchen table contained their words, as if Oliver wasn't in the world at all, let alone just a few feet away.

Oliver heard them, though. He didn't dare speak, and he looked down the moment that one of the adults looked away from the table. But he listened intently to things he didn't quite understand. There were names he'd never heard, and tales he had no context for. He listened to the allusions despite not having the references. He listened to their concerns despite not knowing what warranted the worry. Some things he would piece together in later years; other things would be forgotten before he understood what he was forgetting. But he wasn't the child of anyone in that house, and he had no room of his own. His presence was quickly forgotten by the seaside villagers, who had far greater things to be considering.

"I should 'ave known. I should 'ave told them not to go out this morning." May shook her head. She held her teacup in two hands and sipped it slow. The tea would have gone cold an hour ago, but the tall brown bottle on the table had been tippled into her mug more than once.

"You couldn't have known the weather'd turn, May," Irene said.

Elizabeth nodded. "Or that they'd go out past the third shoal."

May shook her head. "There was a knock," she said.

"Go on with that foolishness." Elizabeth brushed her hand at the air.

"I heard it. I did, Liza," May said. I heard it just as clear as I hears you now."

"Lots of things knock, May."

"No, no. Not like this."

"You know, I couldn't tell you why, but I was some happy when Art said he was gonna stay ashore this mornin'," Irene said.

Elizabeth glared across the table at her.

Irene looked down.

"I should have told my Bobby," May said. "I should have told him when I heard the knock. It was coming right down the stairs."

Aubrey huffed but said nothing, still pretending he wasn't paying attention to the women's conversation. He reached for the bottle.

"Even if I had told him I'd heard it. I didn't need to tell him not to go. I could 'ave just told him what I'd heard. Maybe he'd have thought to be a bit more careful."

"Sure," Elizabeth said. "If I told Aub about every sound I heard around here, I'd never stop talking."

Aubrey clicked his tongue. Arthur gave a half smile. Neither spoke.

"No, it wasn't like that," May said. "There was nothing natural about it. It wasn't the wind or the cold in the house."

"Aye, but you've got seven youngsters," Elizabeth said. "Five of 'em runnin' around."

"There wasn't a soul awake. It was just me. I was adding a bit of wood to the fire before I went back up to bed. And it came right down the stairs."

Aubrey huffed louder this time. He reached for the bottle again, this time tipping it into Arthur's mug.

"It started right at the very top." May wrapped a knuckle against the table. "And I didn't think nothing of it. Houses all make sounds, and like you said, one of the youngsters could have gotten out of bed. But it came again then. Just a bit further down the stairs, and then again, and again. I looked, 'cause I t'ought maybe one of the kids was coming down the stairs, walkin' hard on their heels like I tells 'em not to. But no one was there."

"Not anyone you could see," Irene said.

May nodded. "Not one thing, so far as my eyes could tell. But I tell you, I was looking right at those stairs, and the knock came again. It came the whole way down the stairs, like someone had rolled an alley right off the top step. It knocked right down to the bottom."

"Token. That's a token if I ever heard tell of one," Irene said, loud.

Aubrey tried to cut in. "Don't go talkin' about tokens. It was just a sound, and it's just a storm—"

"Did it come across ya?" Irene asked. "Did you feel it at the bottom of the stairs."

"I don't know. I s'pose I might have."

"A cold shiver. Did you get a shiver?"

"You know what, now that you says it, I did too."

Elizabeth groaned and got up, filling the kettle again.

"It came right across me, like a cold breeze come right through the room."

"A draft," Aubrey said.

"Ten years in that house I've never felt nar draft there."

As May spoke, the wind tore all the way through the house. The edge of the tablecloth, freshly laid before May arrived, was caught in the gust and billowed. There was banging at the door as it swung open.

Oliver jumped up onto the bed. Tucking his legs underneath him. The adults all looked at the door.

"Bobby!" May said in a sharp breath out. But her face fell before the second syllable had fully left her lips. Reality reaffirming itself. Irene put a hand on her arm.

A large figure stood in the doorway. Heavy coat turned up all along the collar, salt-and-pepper cap pulled tight and low over his face. The man pulled the door closed behind him as he scuffed his boots against the worn mat.

Irene tutted and huffed through closed lips. She shifted in her seat and looked at her tea. May looked a little longer at the door but then turned away herself.

Elizabeth didn't look at the figure in the doorway. She spoke to the kitchen sink. "Do you want a cup of tea?"

"Aye, ta," the man said, single syllables coming out muddled. He removed his hat and shook the water from it onto the mat before taking his jacket off his shoulders. "I appreciate ye 'avin' me." The words came out louder, an obvious effort to be clear.

He looked towards the adults at the table and nodded to each of the people sitting there. He touched his forehead, where his hat would have been if it weren't clutched in his hand, when he nodded to the women. The man looked at Oliver and, to the boy's surprise, gave a slight smile, a nod and a touch to his imaginary hat, as if Oliver were worthy of some kind of acknowledgement despite his youth.

The man's voice was thick and heavy. Oliver hadn't heard an accent like his before. He hadn't seen the man's face before either. Not even in church, and in church is where he saw anyone he didn't see about the town or on the wharves.

"There's some ol' black rum there," Aubrey said, looking briefly towards the man.

"Aye, tea will do fer now, thank ye."

Aubrey looked around the kitchen. "Liza, is there e'er chair 'round—"

"Nay. I'm alright. I'm no stranger to standing. Yer window looks inviting." The man's *R*s had a rough roll to them that Oliver found hard to understand. The man made his way to the window in the corner of the living room.

The lantern placed on the window ledge pointed out towards the harbour. It'd be near impossible to see the light through the rain. But it burned there anyway. Many like it were burning in other windows all along the harbour.

The man didn't make conversation with anyone. He didn't even look back towards the company. He took position at the window, and after a moment, he shivered, as if the warmth was just getting to him. As if he were shaking off a cold that had settled deep.

The table returned to conversation, first between Aubrey and Arthur, and then whispers between the women. Oliver watched the new character at the window. His form was more intriguing than the conversation the other adults had returned to. His silence more inviting than their words, which seemed to pretend Oliver didn't exist.

The kettle whistled. Oliver looked over as Elizabeth got up to take it from the stove, speaking as she did so. She poured a mug of black tea then moved back to her seat and outstretched her arm. She didn't look at Oliver, just held out her hand with the mug of tea in his general direction. Oliver stared at the cup for a moment before recognizing his role in the moment. He quickly jumped to his feet and scurried to his aunt, taking the tea from her gingerly, holding it in two hands.

Oliver walked to the window carefully, eyes on the liquid in his hands. He reached the man and stood with feet together, still staring at the tea. The man didn't move. His face was close to the pane, straining to see past his own expression. Oliver opened his mouth and then closed it again, quickly realizing he wasn't equipped with the words for such an interaction. He shuffled a little closer to the man, hoping to alert him to his presence, but the large form remained still.

"Martin," Elizabeth said, loud and sharp with a definitive finish.

The man at the window turned back towards the kitchen table and realized with a start that Oliver was just beside him.

"Aye, ta, Liza," he said.

Martin looked down at Oliver and reached out with both hands, as if encouraged to be gentle by Oliver's delicate grasp.

"Ta, son," he said.

Oliver said nothing but watched as the man's large hands enveloped the teacup and brought it up to his mouth. He took the slightest sip, as if too polite to be concerned with the heat. He looked back down and seemed surprised that Oliver still stood there.

"Now, it's been some time, but surely not enough for you to be May and Bobby's boy?"

Oliver shook his head. May and Bobby's youngest son was a child in a crib, but amongst the older siblings was a boy of four who had straight blond hair. Oliver couldn't possibly be either, and in the back of his mind, he wondered why the man seemed to know nothing of his nephews.

"Good. It's best they're home in bed." He looked back towards the window. A frown set itself deeply into his face, caving in the corners of his mouth, puckering out his bottom lip and tightening the muscles of his jaw as he clenched his teeth together. "Loss is hard to wake up to," he said softly. "But uncertainty is harder to sleep through."

Oliver glanced at the kitchen table, but the other adults hadn't heard Martin's words. Although he was relieved by this, he wasn't certain why it was best the man wasn't heard.

"Who knit ye then?" Martin said, returning to the moment, the distraction at hand.

Oliver hesitated. He hadn't expected the question, the interest in himself. He opened his mouth and closed it, realizing for the second time in the same situation that, unaccustomed to his identity being uncertain, he didn't know the appropriate thing to say. He had never needed to tell anyone who he was. The adults all knew more of his story than he did, and his peers had always been told who he was by their parents. Salvage isn't a big place, and strangers aren't common. Only the ministers came and went, but even they had been told who Oliver was long before he had ever sat in their pews.

"Well, news often takes its time reaching my part of the shore, but I don't believe Elizabeth and Aubrey ever had a youngster. Or have they?"

Oliver looked down, his gaze hooked on the uneven floorboards. He shook his head.

Martin watched the boy for a moment, wondering if any words would follow. He said nothing for some time, thinking that the boy would move along, that he was present out of politeness, not interest. Martin chewed his bottom lip for a moment. He pretended to look past their reflections again, to the sea churning in autumn's anger.

"You know, I've seen you before," Martin said.

Oliver's back straightened a little, the slightest tilt of curiosity in his head.

"I've seen you down the shore, down my way." Martin sipped from his tea and added, "I've seen you diving off the rocks. You're quite the swimmer."

Oliver's big brown eyes expanded and instantly began to glisten; his face paled and elongated. He looked down again and shook his head gently.

"Aye. Yer just like a fish, lad . . . Or a seal, perhaps." Martin looked at Oliver again, but the boy hadn't lifted his gaze from the floorboards. Martin sipped from his tea, his expression suggesting his acceptance that he would never hear the boy utter a word.

But Oliver then stuttered a very quiet "Sir?"

He turned towards the window, encouraging Martin to recognize that he wanted his words to go unnoticed by the others.

"Please," Oliver said, "could you not tell Aunt Elizabeth, or Uncle Aubrey, that you seen me swimming?"

"Aye, so, its aunt and uncle, is it?" Martin nodded slow and took another sip of his tea. "Are ye one of Aubrey's crowd then? Saunders blood?"

Oliver shook his head.

"Ahh, right." Martin nodded with an understanding.

Oliver nodded back. "They wouldn't like it," he said, "if they knew I'd been out swimming. If they knew you'd seen me."

Martin smiled with half of his mouth. "Son, it'd be much worse for me than ye if yer aunt and uncle knew I'd seen ye swimming in the sea all by yerself."

Oliver looked at the man, his eyebrows pressing towards his nose.

"It's not something you're old enough to understand."

Air escaped Martin's nose in a long hiss, and his jaw clenched hard enough that Oliver could watch the man's cheeks quiver.

"But ye know, son, I'm yet to see years make a man more understanding."

"Aunt Elizabeth told me that I'm not allowed to swim. Uncle Aubrey," he added more quietly, "he says I can't go swimming either, but he says that no one knows if no one sees."

"And why do you think he says that?"

Oliver shrugged. "He says that people don't understand why I likes the water." His words grew quieter as his sentence ended, like his faith in his ability to speak couldn't make it all the way to the last syllable.

"There's probably some truth in what your uncle told ye. People, especially around here, expect things to be a certain way. They're awful wary of it when it's different. As quick as the sea can change, the folks that live off it are slow to take to difference." Martin had a sad smile for a moment. "Here I am, telling ye that yer too young to understand when grown folks not understanding is the reason it needs any explaining at all. It's been much the same for me, son. Just different ways."

Martin looked at the boy from the corner of his eye for a long moment, considering continuing, weighing the value of an explanation. He looked back out the window.

"Don't worry," he said. "I won't tell your aunt, nor your uncle, that I saw you swimming. But you'd best keep a closer eye on the shore before you leave it. It's easier to go unseen than to try give an explanation."

Oliver looked up with wide eyes and a relieved smile.

"Your mother liked the water too. And I 'magine she could swim just as well as you can."

Oliver's mouth opened, but no sound escaped.

"You're Albert and Georgia's son, aren't ye?"

The boy nodded quick and hard.

"Aye, you have your mother's eyes. Her love for the sea too."

Oliver held his breath. He couldn't remember his mother's eyes, let alone that they might have resembled his. "You knew her?" he said quietly.

The man nodded, slow and methodical. "Not well. Nay, I wouldn't think that anyone knew her well. But I was there the night they met, you know."

Oliver's smile spilled over. He had heard his father's name over his aunt's lips on a handful of occasions, but no one had ever spoken of his mother, let alone how she had met his father.

Martin couldn't help but smile back at the boy, "Oh, my son, what a night it was."

Oliver was told a story then. He was told a story of a night with a full moon, and thick fog. A story of a party and a parting dance floor. Of young love and youthful beauty. Of passion and desire's deliverance. He was told a story of two people he had no memory of meeting, but who represented an idea that meant more to him than he knew how to express.

Blast

The repercussion of an encounter with a fairy, often an abnormally presenting injury or infection.

Sundays are still, in Salvage. The boats don't leave their moorings; the fisherman do no busy work at the wharves. The tides still rise and fall, but no matter how fair the weather or how full the seas, the sanctity of the day is not tested. Men who challenge the nor'easter gales, who brashly refuse to heed the warning of a morning's bright red sky, will not wet their lines on even the most pleasant Sunday morning. There are some forces that even those men won't challenge, some things that warrant more fear than even the sea.

Although the midafternoon sun was warm on the skin, a steady breeze came in off the sea. Oliver sat in the sunshine on the porch of his aunt and uncle's home. His stomach was full. Salt beef had been left in a pot, covered in cabbage and root vegetables, and boiled while they'd gone to church. After the Jiggs' dinner, the three changed out of their Sunday best. Aubrey had taken to his chair in the parlour, letting sleep find its way to him. Oliver and his aunt both took to the sunshine.

"Some day on clothes," Elizabeth said, to no one in particular.

A long wooden pole was propped up at one end of the garden; thick fishing leader was strung between the house and the pole. No clothing hung from that line. Oliver imagined the way that the wind would catch the material and billow it outwards, testing the strength of the clothespins as it exposed every inch of their clothes to the sky. Between the sun and the wind, the clothing would dry quickly. But on Sundays, not even laundry could be done. Elizabeth longed to take advantage of the day, but if her own beliefs didn't stop her, the reprimand she would receive from neighbours did.

Oliver looked up at his aunt as she spoke. She didn't smile, but there was a contentedness about her as she tilted her head back, eyes closed, absorbing the sun. Oliver was toying with the frayed pieces of an old net. One knot at a time, he returned strength to the webbing. It was a retired net, not needed for the season, so Oliver's actions didn't feel like real work. Real net work wouldn't be done on Sunday, nor would it be entrusted to a fourteen-year-old boy. But even if it were, the fishermen weren't likely to offer it to Oliver Brown.

He could hear distant laughter, broken by the breeze, blown across the yard by the ocean wind. A little way up the shore, on the other side of the road, Oliver could see May Ryan in the garden. Her youngest children scurried around her feet, creating some kind of game in the sunshine.

It had been almost five years since her husband hadn't returned. Weeks later, some ocean-weathered wood was found washed ashore. It could have been part of Bobby's boat, but the planks, thrashed and cracked from crashing into shoals and shore, only served to snuff out hope that had already been lost. Broken boards didn't comfort anyone as to how the end may have come, so no one took the time to confirm or negate the origin of the wood. When the sea steals, it consumes. What isn't swallowed whole is chewed up.

The youngest of the Ryan children had no memory of their father. Perhaps that's why their laughter could be carried down the shore: they didn't have a memory to miss. May smiled at her children now, but recent years had carved deep lines in her face. Oliver did not envy May's pain, but he pitied the children who wouldn't know whose features they'd inherited. They would never know which of their mannerisms were a product of someone else's nature. He hoped they'd have stories—from siblings, from their mother—of the man they 'longed to.

Oliver looked away from the family and past his aunt, back out at the water. The sunlight caught the gentle ripples, and the water's surface was a shimmering reflection of the blue sky above.

"Fair day," Oliver said, echoing his aunt's sentiment minutes after she'd spoken.

"Yuh," Elizabeth said with an inhale.

Oliver took a deep breath. The kind of breath that fills the bottom of the lungs and refreshes something other than oxygen deep inside. He let out a gentle and satisfied sigh.

Then he heard the crunching of feet on gravel just beneath the sound of lapping waves and turned to see Johnathan Genge making his way down the dirt road. Oliver allowed himself a smile while Johnathan was still too far away to see his face.

It had been three years and a season since Johnathan had fallen from the ice pans. The boy had spent weeks in bed, trying to get the chill out of his bones. Despite Johnathan being dry in bed, it had been uncertain for quite some time if his encounter with the water would claim his life. No one spoke about the events of that day anymore—not when Oliver was around, at least. Some folks had patted him on the back that afternoon and over the couple days that followed. Johnathan's mother had thanked him, but with reservation in her appreciation. People were uncomfortable with Oliver's health, the way the ocean didn't seem to claw away at his life. Elizabeth had kept Oliver inside for a couple days after, but he hadn't needed the time spent by the fire the way that Johnathan had.

That story, like most stories around the harbour, became more of a telling than a happening. People would preface the tale with affirmation of its reality, but their choice of what details to include forever influenced what would be forgotten. They chose which details were worth accentuating and exaggerating, and as parts of the story grew uncertain, the right questions led to fabricated answers. With every retelling, it became more of a story. Recounting lost its importance until the tale was held in higher regard than reality.

It became less about the saving of Johnathan Genge and more about the actions of Oliver. While Oliver's actions and Johnathan's saving had once been one and the same, now the focus fell on how long both boys had been submerged and the distance they'd apparently swum in the icy waters. Oliver was never asked about the event: but he wasn't asked about many things, no matter how directly they pertained to him. Perhaps the story would be ruined if he offered a different narrative than the one they'd come to tell. Perhaps Oliver's story would have been precisely the story they whispered over bonfires. But uncertainty makes a rumour more exciting than truth ever could.

Johnathan had no memory of being rescued. He claimed that he remembered losing his balance, and a sharp pain as the back of his head struck the ice. But he didn't find consciousness again until days later. Of course, he was told that Oliver was involved in his rescue, but he could have attributed that to luck, as many people in the community had. Perhaps some part of him knew it was more than happenstance or good fortune that led to his rescue. Or perhaps the moment on the ice had nothing to do with his attitude.

Whatever the case, over the first few years that followed, Johnathan found kindness for Oliver. None of his gestures were grandiose—they were barely noticed by other people—but to Oliver, Johnathan's passive kindness was like the warmth of low tide's turning. The simple absence of cruelty that Johnathan offered was enough for him to be the sole occupant of the word "friend" in Oliver's mind.

Johnathan's mind didn't seem to be anywhere near ice pans and injury now. He walked along the gravel road, kicking at loose stones with lightness in his step. His direction brought him past Elizabeth and Aubrey's house. He looked at Oliver and smiled, giving him a half wave. Oliver returned the smile and held up his own hand, attempting to be casual.

One day not long after Johnathan had healed and escaped his bed, the children of Salvage had all been walking in the sunshine on their way home from the schoolhouse. Oliver was behind the other children. He no longer tried to keep up and had come to accept his exclusion. But on this day, without any comment, Johnathan had slowed his own walk. Eventually, Oliver caught up to him and looked at the boy with curiosity, but Johnathan said nothing. He only matched Oliver's pace, and they walked home together. Oliver had come to relish those silent walks, and this unspoken companionship was the first companionship he'd known.

Before he disappeared from Oliver's line of sight, Johnathan gave a nod of his head in the direction he was travelling. A simple head tilt, accompanied by a grin. Oliver nodded, still smiling brightly, and dropped the piece of old net.

"Where are you off to then?" Elizabeth said, opening her eyes for a moment.

"Down the road," he said.

Elizabeth looked at him a moment and nodded, turning her head back towards the sky.

Johnathan stood waiting for him. Together, the two boys walked away from the houses of Salvage towards the woods on the hillside.

It wasn't the first time that Oliver and Johnathan had spent time together beyond their silent walks home from school. It wasn't frequent, but they had kept each other company on a handful of occasions.

Soon they were beyond the sight of the town, and their strides seemed to drift closer together. Oliver found himself looking down at their feet, and then at Johnathan's gently swinging arms. Their feet seemed to be searching for the same steps. As if by accident, Oliver let his finger graze Johnathan's hand. A couple paces later, Oliver felt Johnathan's hand touch his own. The touch was brief and unmentioned, but Oliver could feel warmth spread across his cheeks. His ears were hot and he could hear his heart. He reached out more confidently and let his fingers find his friend's. Oliver's smile grew to show every tooth in his head, but he kept his gaze down. The contact was gentle, but the boys kept their hands together, making more and more contact with each pace until they were interlaced. When the spaces between fingers were entirely filled with each other's, Oliver gave a gentle squeeze. Johnathan squeezed back hard enough that it almost hurt and then let go, using both hands to give Oliver a shove.

The push forced Oliver a couple paces away, but he leaned into his shoulder and fell back towards Johnathan, colliding with him and sending the boy in the other direction. They both laughed and continued walking. It wasn't the first time their fingers had found each other. It was something that just happened sometimes when they were alone together, away from everyone else.

Oliver hadn't paid much attention to where they were walking. He tried to reach again for his friend's hand, but this time Johnathan pulled away. He pushed his hands into his pockets and added a little space between them. He did this sometimes. Oliver craved the boy's touch, but Johnathan wasn't always willing to give it. Oliver could never predict when he would squeeze back and when he would push him away, so he just tried, and hoped.

Johnathan was a few paces away now. He took a left-hand turn off the route. Oliver didn't immediately follow. He stood still on the main trail, watching as Johnathan followed a small footpath through a wooden gate.

Johnathan stopped just on the other side of the fence. He looked back at Oliver, smiling and tilting his head, an instruction to follow.

Oliver ground the toe of his boot into the gravel and looked at the mark he'd made on the path as if it was remarkably interesting. When he drew his eyes from the dirt, he didn't look directly at Johnathan but beyond him, to the cluttered combination of grey gravestones and white crosses that covered the ground.

"Come on," Johnathan said.

He gestured with his head to the far side of the graveyard, where no one bothered to upkeep the fence and the forest was taking back the cleared land. It was a secluded area, out of sight of the path.

Johnathan saw Oliver's eyes roaming the stones.

"You haven't been in here?" he said.

Oliver shook his head.

Johnathan looked down for a moment, and he plucked a piece

of tall grass from the earth just outside the cemetery. He stuck the grass in his mouth and began chewing on it. He turned and looked around the graveyard, not moving any further away from Oliver.

Oliver scanned the bushes for a tall piece of yellow grass like Johnathan had, but the only grass near him was too green or too brown. He took a few steps forward, not passing the threshold of the cemetery but getting close enough to his friend to pluck his own piece of grass.

"Is this where they are?" Johnathan asked with a nonchalance that only youth allows.

Oliver shrugged.

"Sure, they ain't gonna hurt ya."

"I know," Oliver shot back.

"I mean, why would they, right?"

Oliver shrugged.

Johnathan stepped out of the graveyard and stood closer to Oliver. He kicked at the ground by the boy's toes, as if trying to knock free his anchored feet.

"He's not even there, is he?"

Oliver shook his head.

"So, you may as well go see where he's not!"

Oliver shrugged, and Johnathan grabbed his hand from where it hung from his side, towing the boy through the gate.

Despite his discomfort, Oliver found himself grinning at the contact again. He allowed himself to be pulled into the graveyard. Johnathan led him through the uneven rows, and they read each name silently as they passed.

Oliver told himself that he wasn't looking for anything; he wasn't sure if there would be anything to see even if he were.

"Luh," Johnathan said. He raised their linked hands towards a faded gravestone.

Oliver could barely make out the name. He didn't recognize it.

"That's your grandfather, isn't it?"

Oliver shrugged. He didn't know if this was his grandfather or not.

Johnathan nodded and let go of Oliver's hand, proceeding deeper into the small cemetery. "He was your grandmudder Margret's husband," he said.

Oliver looked after his friend and then back at the gravestone. He had never met his grandmother. He knew she lived down the road from Elizabeth and Aubrey. Elizabeth spoke of her occasionally, but only ever to Aubrey. What Oliver knew of the women had been collected from snippets of sentences overheard, but it was never information offered to him. Oliver saw the elderly lady in church sometimes, but she'd never looked at him.

Johnathan had wandered ahead while Oliver stood looking at his grandfather's grave. Johnathan was moving towards the far side of the graveyard where the fence had fallen into disrepair, where the headstones were the most weathered. Where the two boys would be out of the eye lines of the main trail.

Oliver followed his companion slowly, reading names as he went. He spent time looking at each headstone and cross, which meant nothing to him. It seemed polite, at first, to pay attention to the names of the people they walked above, but now he read the stones to slow his walk.

Johnathan stopped walking and leaned against a rock that was too large to have been removed and had stayed as it was surrounded by carved and polished versions of itself. Johnathan stared at a gravestone. He glanced back at Oliver and then pointed at the stone.

Oliver stopped moving. He felt his feet take root in the earth. The soles of his shoes were sinking. Imperceptible hands were reaching up from the dirt and clutching at his ankles, holding him in place.

"Wanna go up the hill?" Oliver asked. He turned and looked behind them: at the trail, at an escape, at all the places that weren't where they stood.

"Just come look."

"Nah." Oliver kept his head turned away, not sure why he didn't want to look. He wasn't sure why his feet were in such agreement with his reservations.

Both boys were silent. For the first time since he'd begun walking with Johnathan, Oliver realized that he couldn't feel the breeze off the water. The hillside and the firs that surrounded the cemetery kept the salt-water air from reaching him. All at once he felt suffocated, his stomach knotted in discomfort. He wanted to run away. He wanted to run back to the shore.

"Oliver," Johnathan said softly. "Oliver, not looking don't mean it's not here."

Oliver looked at the other boy curiously, taken aback.

That was the first time Johnathan had ever said his name. It had been an absence in their interactions that Oliver hadn't realized until then. The sound of his name on his friend's lips swept over his skin, raising tiny hairs and leaving ripples like a cool salt-water breeze. He took a deep breath.

Slowly, Oliver stepped forward. The years of exposure were as easy to read as the dates engraved. This piece of stone hadn't been expensive, but it was more than many empty graves received. Oliver knew that the graveyard was filled with lots of empty graves, many from years ago when men left to fight in the east and only letters returned. War was a distant place where men were turned into memories, as far as Oliver understood. The cemetery had more empty graves from bodies taken by the sea than bodies left on the other side of it. But storms don't send letters home or encourage plaques in the ground. Oliver's father's body missing from that graveyard was a matter of safety and cost over anything else. No one wanted to bring a body taken by consumption back into the town, or at least no one wanted to pay for it.

"In loving memory of Albert Brown," it read. "Beloved Father, Nephew and Son." Beneath the dates, it declared his age as twenty-four.

"It doesn't say your mum's name," Johnathan said quietly. "Or even 'husband.'" Even his whisper sounded loud in the boys' extended silence. "That's probably just because it was too much."

"Probably," Oliver said. He didn't mention that it didn't say his name either. The other stones mentioned the family members who mourned, but those Albert Brown left behind weren't named.

Johnathan put his arm over Oliver's shoulder with rough affection. He bent his arm at the elbow, hooking it around Oliver's neck, and put his hands together, squeezing him in a mock headlock for a moment. Oliver didn't move and Johnathan let go. He left his arm around Oliver's shoulders for a moment before running his hand over the back of Oliver's neck. Fingers passing through the hair on the back of his head, ruffling it gently. And then Johnathan let his hand slide down the boy's back, gentle contact getting lighter and lighter until his touch disappeared.

Johnathan leaned back against the large rock.

With a sigh, Oliver fell back beside him.

Immediately, Johnathan placed his hand on Oliver's thigh.

"Haven't you been here before?" Johnathan asked, knowing the answer.

Oliver said nothing. He looked at Johnathan's hand on his thigh.

"Did you know this was here?"

Oliver shrugged. "I knew something was here."

"But you never comes up to visit? My fadder comes to visit his mum all the time." Johnathan turned around, looking back over the cemetery at a place where a relative he'd never known had been buried.

"He isn't actually here," Oliver said.

It seemed like the acceptable thing to say. But when he was a boy, no one had ever brought him here. By the time he was old enough to have figured out where it was, he'd convinced himself it didn't matter. And perhaps it didn't matter, he thought. Not much matters when you're a kid, especially things you can't even remember.

"I'm sorry," Johnathan said. "I shouldn't have made you come here." He squeezed Oliver's thigh.

"I thought she was here, too," Oliver said quietly.

A blank space was next to the empty grave of his father. But nothing was there, no stone or cross. The earth itself looked untouched. Two spaces where the earth had never been turned.

Oliver's stomach was tightening and twisting. He was uncomfortable with the cemetery, with the moment, and pulled away from his leaning place. He felt overwhelmed. He grabbed Johnathan's hand from his thigh but kept hold of it.

Johnathan kept his feet planted. As Oliver tried to pull him away, he pulled back. He smiled brightly at Oliver, encouraging him to try again, for a competition to begin.

Oliver gave half a smile and let go. He turned away and began walking further into the cemetery.

Things aren't forgotten all at once. A memory isn't visited one day and gone the next. You need to forget to visit it before you can forget it altogether. Graves aren't so different. When they're not visited enough, they begin to decay, and nature takes back the once tamed ground. It takes a town to forget a grave, though; any visitor can keep it remembered for any other. To forget a memory only takes a boy, only time.

As Oliver walked further from the graveyard's entrance, nature's endeavours to take back the ground became more prominent. Some stones were so faded they were hardly more than rocks, and the tall grass that surrounded them hid them from sight. Further still, alder bushes and the beginnings of firs had claimed the land. Where there had once been a fence, there was now fallen wood, rotting and feeding that which grew in its place.

The line between graveyard and forest wasn't clear where Oliver stood. He could no longer see the remnants of the fence, painted such a bright white when the cemetery opened. Now only the absence of grown trees alluded to what was once cared for. He slowed his pace. He wasn't sure what he was walking towards, or away from. Perhaps he had heard a whisper, a passing reference long ago that subconsciously guided him. Or perhaps something else entirely was pulling him to that place. With feet stilled, he scanned the low-lying foliage until he found what he hadn't known he was searching for. A wooden cross, faded to a weathered grey not unlike the rotting fence, stood askew only a few paces away.

"Let's 'ead back to the path," Johnathan called. His voice was distant; he hadn't followed Oliver so far into the overgrown gravesite.

Oliver walked forward until he stood facing the cross, tilted and rotting in the ground. It had no name and was hardly recognizable as a marker. But in front of the cross, instead of alder bushes and tall grass, was a thick bed of thistles.

"Let's go back," Johnathan said again, closer this time.

Oliver turned to find the boy not far behind him, speaking softly.

"Look," Oliver said.

"I don't like how it's all grown in here. It's not natural. It 'appened too fast."

Oliver looked at Johnathan with curiosity. He couldn't understand how the boy could call nature unnatural. No matter how fast it happened, if it happened, then surely it's natural. He looked back at the thistles in front of him.

"I think this is her," he said.

Johnathan sighed and Oliver heard the crunching of the grass under his feet as he crept further forward. His footsteps sounded loud in the quiet of the woods.

"There isn't any stone," Oliver said. "Or any name."

"There wouldn't be though, would there. Not with the way she went and all."

Oliver nodded. "That's why she's all the way over here."

Johnathan didn't say anything, but he did not step away. Both boys stood staring at what might have been the grave of someone neither of them knew. Oliver felt Johnathan's fingers on his own then, felt their hands tie gently together. He was comforted by his friend's presence. Comforted by someone else being nearby. He wished then that his mother wasn't buried so far away from everyone else. Even if the townsfolk didn't like her much, surely some people would be better than no one. She must be so lonely there, all alone. She'd be lonely there forevermore. Oliver felt hot tears on his cheeks. He wiped them away quickly, onto the shoulder of his shirt.

"Let's go," Johnathan said. "If the woods is taking back the graveyard that fast, there must be fairies around." He poked Oliver in the side, adding a jest to his words.

Johnathan didn't really fear the fairies. He wouldn't admit to it even if he did. Stories of fairies were told to children to keep them away from dangerous areas of the land. Some adults stood hard alongside claims of sightings, or even attacks, with the proof being supplied by inexplicable wounds or strange occurrences in the environment. But most children grew out of the stories, no longer expecting the short, almost human-looking creatures to be lurking throughout the woods.

Oliver barely heard Johnathan's playful reference to the fairy myths. He was too caught up in the real grave before him.

"Perhaps the flowers keep her company," Oliver said quietly, not intending for even Johnathan to hear. But the forest had grown so quiet that his voice carried across the graveyard.

"Maybe." Johnathan reached out as if to pick one of the purple thistle heads, but instead he only brushed his fingertips against it, holding its weight for a moment before letting go.

There was a distant rustling in the trees, likely a bird, or maybe a hare. But both boys were suddenly staring into the woods. Both of them were acutely aware of the silence all around them. Oliver looked back. The walk in had been made stone by stone, and he hadn't noticed the distance that it had added up to. His father's gravestone was further away than he had expected it to be, the path out of the cemetery and back to the trail even further.

Johnathan moved from Oliver's side. He kept his proximity but changed his positioning until he stood between Oliver and the denseness of the woods. Oliver looked at Johnathan quizzically for a moment, curious about the boy's protective positioning. But a smile snuck over Johnathan's face—a grin, just for a moment—that alerted Oliver to his game of pretend.

"Are you getting scared of the woods, Johnny Genge?" Oliver asked, smiling up at him.

Johnathan shuffled even closer to him. "No, I figured you might be worried about the fairies though. Still being a youngster and all."

Oliver snorted. "What's the matter. Nar bread crumb in your pockets?"

"I haven't." Johnathan smiled. "But I wish I had. It'd make saving us easy." He brought his shoulder up broad and wide, as if preparing to fight off the forewarned creatures.

A crow cawed sharp and loud in the dense woods not far away, as if it was shocked to find visitors there. Or like visitors had only just arrived. When its bark fell silent, Oliver felt the forest's quiet somehow deeper than before. It was like all the animals wouldn't dare to make a sound. It wasn't just a silence to the ears now; it was a quiet that encapsulated their bodies.

Johnathan shuffled his way a little closer to Oliver. There seemed to be anxiousness hidden beneath his smile and behind his red cheeks. Oliver realized his own face was flushed too as he stared at his friend's firming jawline and proudly growing, patchy stubble. And then from blushing cheeks to his red lips, not so far away.

"We'll have to stay close together to look stronger," Johnathan said, letting his hips knock against Oliver's. "Like we're just one thing that's too big to be hurt by their blasts." His eyes glanced back and forth from the forest to Oliver's lips, then less the afore and more the after.

Oliver could feel his friend's breath against his face. It was close. It was warm. Oliver's eyes met Johnathan's for a moment before they both looked at each other's lips. Oliver felt the boy's fingers along his shirt buttons, feeling the seam. Johnathan's other hand had fallen to the edge of Oliver's front pocket.

Oliver placed his hand over Johnathan's at his pocket, interlacing their fingers. He left the fingers on his shirt buttons, letting them continue to feel their way up and down. Oliver placed his other hand on his friend's hip.

Oliver felt Johnathan's finger hook in between the buttons of his shirt, the gentle tug forward, pulling him closer. Each boy's gaze danced back and forth between lips and eyes until their faces had grown too close to focus. Their eyes closed.

A branch cracked in the forest.

It was so loud it could have echoed, but the crack was instantly overwhelmed by a chorus of angry chickadees and crows, a torrent of jays and jackdaws. More cracking, snapping and rustling followed, loud and growing closer as something forced its way violently through the undergrowth.

Both boys looked to the forest with held breath, fearing the unknown about to explode through the trees.

Oliver wished it had been a fairy. Something supernatural and sinister from which the boys could have run. It would have become a story to tell in later years. Even if the fairies were as bad as the old folks said, he would have chosen to take his chances.

Instead, the form that burst through the trees wasn't something that could be run from. It was Johnathan's father who crashed through the undergrowth, and his voice boomed so loud that he may as well have been a giant. Johnathan's father had seen the proximity of the boys, and he had seen his son's lips poised before Oliver's. And no matter how quickly the boys ran, they couldn't change that he had seen them.

Johnathan's father didn't understand the beginnings of young love he saw on that summer day. Or perhaps he refused to understand it. His shouts were more than just a reprimanding of romance; they were accusations of perversion and declarations of disgust. His shouts were directed at Oliver, as a source of corruption, trouble and the unnatural. While his father hollered, Johnathan shoved Oliver away. He pushed him hard and rough, and kept his head turned away.

Oliver ran away with tears flowing down his face. He ran from the forest as quickly as he could, wanting only to get back to the sea, back to the coast and the ocean breeze. Oliver ran with fear heating his face before he could feel his exertion. He ran to the water, to the comfort that he knew waited for him there, but as he furthered himself from the bellowing voice of Johnathan's father, he could feel the distance he was creating from Johnathan as well. He could still hear the way his name had sounded on his friend's lips and knew, somehow, that he would never hear Johnathan speak it again.

Skiff

A large, partly decked fishing boat used during the coastal fishery.

Salvage doesn't slope gently into the sea. The land ends in stone: jagged, uneven and sharp. There is no flat ground to place a floor upon, or earth in which to embed a foundation. The sea sucked away the soil long ago, and the waves battered and broke the shorelines, leaving only the hardened and the lasting. Settlers to this coast did not conquer it; they did not break away the rocks and reshape the land. They chose to cope instead of conquer, doing their best with what the land offered, inhabiting the harsh place for the fruits of the sea. Houses were built simple, propped up on the rocks, supported by stilts. To build something resembling their old world that could withstand the ocean would have required resources that none of those first newcomers had. Instead, they built upon rocks that the ocean didn't seem capable of taking.

Now colour splatters along the shorelines, never coating the land but appearing in patches and flecks. Homes are painted bright to battle against the greyness that can take hold of this coast. Greyness had settled here long before England sought sea routes or fish, long before the longboats of the Norse, long before even the Beothuk, who knew these rocky coasts better than anyone who came after. The fog owns these shores more than any human ever could or ever will.

Oliver sat on the edge of the wharf, his legs still, hanging over the grey, weathered wood that had grown soft and feathered from sun and sea. The fog had settled over Salvage. He had watched it roll in, a bank as thick and high as a mountain sliding towards the shore. It wasn't raining, but the air was wet. It was cold and the grey sky spit a fine mist. There wasn't a drop of water to be felt until it had accumulated enough that it rolled off the skin. Oliver's clothes had grown damp. He didn't feel the cold though; he didn't mind the weather. He listened to the waves lapping against the shore, waiting to hear the wet and slippery sounds of fish.

It was capelin weather. They would be rolling soon, pouring onto the beaches up the shore by the thousands, many never to return to the water again. Indifferent to their fate, the capelin come to the beaches to spawn, and as they roll over each other and onto the shore, death becomes nothing but a by-product of procreation.

A church bell rang out behind him. Its sound was heavy and deep, but even the vibration of the brass struggled to cut through the fog. It continued to ring. Oliver knew that somewhere behind him, a group—quickly growing saturated in their best black clothing—would be moving from churchyard to graveyard. Oliver hadn't been invited to the church. It was the funeral of his grandmother, a woman he'd never met the eye of let alone shared a word with.

Oliver wasn't hurt by his lack of inclusion. His grandmother Margret had never accepted him in life, even in sickness. No one had ever spoken directly to him about her disposition towards him. But there had been enough quiet comments from Elizabeth over the years that Oliver knew his grandmother had hated his mother, hated her so much that the feeling seemed to apply to his mother's blood, which flowed in him. He didn't expect that death would give him a place in the world of his grandmother. A place was something he had come to give up searching for.

It had been almost three years since that day in the graveyard. Oliver didn't think of the day often but still thought of it more often than he wanted to. The words of Johnathan's father were still too loud. He could still feel them cutting what had existed between him and his only friend. He could still feel how quickly the other boy's fingers had left his own. The forcefulness with which Johnathan had shoved him away, the fear he'd worn on his face, the anger on his father's.

The story of that day did not spread. For that, Oliver was thankful. The people of the town had already looked at him from the corners of their eyes. They already turned their backs to him and spoke of him behind closed doors. But Johnathan's father had feared for his son's involvement in the moment and therefore said nothing. Johnathan hadn't spoken to Oliver since. At the schoolhouse, Oliver saw the heavily bruised side of Johnathan's face for the next few days. Oliver felt those bruises as much as Johnathan. He hated himself for a long while, believing those bruises were there because of him, too young to understand that he wasn't responsible for the violent actions of another, no matter the inspiration of such violence. Oliver would steal glances at Johnathan when he could, when no one was looking, when he wouldn't be noticed. But Oliver didn't try to speak to him, not wanting Johnathan to be hurt anymore. As lonely as it was to be on the outskirts, he didn't wish it upon another.

Johnathan went with Rebecca Smith now. Rebecca was Missy

Smith's daughter, so Oliver had watched her grow up as his neighbour. He thought she was a kind girl, mostly because she lacked the meanness that Oliver felt from many of his peers. She looked at Johnathan the same way that Oliver did, but she didn't need to hide her admiration. They'd been going together for almost a year. Oliver watched many times as Johnathan walked along the same road that he used to join him on—past his house and on to hers—and now she joined him instead. They'd be married soon. Everyone said that. Rebecca had never been cruel to Oliver. But for all her kindness, Oliver couldn't bring himself to like her. Oliver was not accustomed to disliking people. It wasn't in his nature. He hated the way that he felt towards the girl, who had never done anything wrong. But his muscles stiffened when he saw the two together.

Oliver did wish, sometimes, that he could go back to that graveyard again. He wished that he could see the earth beneath which his mother had been laid. But for some reason, he didn't believe the thistles would be there anymore. He couldn't bring himself to return, to risk seeing Johnathan's father. To walk in the memory of a moment that had made him feel so many different things.

From where he was sitting on the wharf, Oliver heard the thick puttering of a single-cylinder motor through the fog. The grey was too thick to reveal where the boat was. It would be upon him before he could see it. But as it grew closer, Oliver heard a splashing that didn't match a boat cutting through the water. He could hear voices, fast and panicked, just beneath the motorboat's sound and realized the boat was heading directly for him.

He jumped to his feet, eyes straining to see through the mist. There was a commotion on the coming boat, something not right, something inspiring alarm. Then Oliver saw the bow through the fog. It was low in the water, far too low. He saw the dark green oils of the men onboard. Two were furiously bailing, tossing buckets of water over either side of the boat. Oliver recognized Barry Newport on the tiller, guiding the boat straight towards the wharf. He was knee deep in water; the aft of the boat was on the cusp of sinking.

"Eh," Oliver called to the men. "Toss me the painter!"

Clyde, the younger of the Newport brothers, looked up at Oliver. The boat was still too far away for the bow rope to be thrown to the dock. The third fisherman didn't look up, bailing so quickly that his sloppy tosses of the bucket were barely useful. He was a young man from two towns over that the brothers had hired, and his greenness showed in his fear. Their progress was painfully slow; the boat seemed to be going down as quickly as it was moving forward. The old make-and-break engine was firing just above the water's surface. For all its might, even that old Acadia couldn't fire under water.

Clyde looked back at Barry, at the water steadily rising. They were only twenty yards from the dock. Clyde didn't stop bailing as he contemplated.

Oliver stepped to the wharf's very edge and stretched his hand out as far as he could, trying to prove that a rope could be thrown the distance.

Decision made, Clyde leapt towards the bow of the boat. With a couple flicks of his wrist, he tied the heavy wooden bailing bucket to the bitter end of the painter. Clyde dropped three feet of line from his right hand and spun the bucket once, twice, around in a fast circle before releasing it with a hard extension of his shoulder.

The bucket hurled towards Oliver, but it was slowed with every inch of rope it pulled from the motorboat's deck. Clyde had hurled it high and far, but even then, the distance seemed vast. Oliver reached as far as he could, but the bucket passed just inches from his hand. As it dropped towards the water, he dropped down as well, and the remaining forward momentum of the throw brought the painter into his grasp. He gripped hard.

He jumped to his feet and began pulling with all his might, arm over arm. The engine puttered, offering all it could, and Oliver offered even more. The three men in the boat tried their hardest to bail her, but the vessel was sinking despite all efforts. It seemed destined to a grave just short of the wharf. Clyde had cupped together his hands, splashing water over the side as the icy Atlantic poured over his thighs The men were close enough that they'd be safe now. They were thinking only about the health of the boat.

"To the slip," Barry called to Oliver. He gestured at the sloped ground—covered in round, smoothed logs—next to the wharf.

Following instructions, Oliver rushed back the length of the wharf, all the while pulling the rope. He jumped to the ground and began dragging the three men into the slip with all his strength. His arms burned, but the muscles of his back were tight and strong, and he was anchored hard. Hand over hand, every foot of progress was a strain, but his young body wouldn't fail him.

The same couldn't be said for the rope.

Too long since it'd last been checked, too many years of sun and salt: the painter snapped. Oliver fell hard onto his back, the back of his trousers ripping on the wood of the slip. By all accounts, the forward momentum of the boat had almost stopped entirely at this point. The single-stroke engine made a pitiful cough as it submerged.

The boat, just off the shore, was only ten feet from being grounded. Clyde was the first to jump out into the chest-deep water, futilely trying to pull the boat forward.

Oliver didn't hesitate. He got up from his backside, where the sudden release had left him, and marched straight into the cold water. His feet were sure on the kelp-coated slip, his balance confident. Once he stood in the water, Oliver could feel the ocean in his very core. He could feel the swell of tons of water moving, of currents flowing, of waves crashing. He could feel the power of the sea as if it was present in his own hands, as if it anchored his feet instead of trying to sweep them away.

When Oliver reached the boat, Barry Newport was scrambling over the side. In his later years, Barry would claim that his hands never even reached the boat's gunwale. He'd claim that the skiff was moving so quickly towards the shore he could hardly keep up to lend a hand. He'd say that he thought he was going to send the boy running, to slam on doors and get more men to help, but then he'd realized that the boy was all the help the boat needed. That's how Barry would tell the story at least, many years later.

The fog, as thick as it was, sealed Oliver and the three fishermen into that moment. For all the homes that lined that harbour, the saltboxes that bordered the very slip they stood upon, not one other soul saw the Newports' boat come in that day. It was the kind of fog that made you lose sight of a door after you'd opened it. The kind of fog that keeps secrets.

The three men on that boat had been bailing water for a mile and half, since they'd struck the shoal. They'd been fighting for their lives, unsure if the rate of water coming in could be overcome by buckets and a single-speed engine. They were exhausted and desperate for land, for hope. They'd claim to remember that day perfectly, to know the exact weight of the water-filled vessel and know for certain how much Oliver Brown had to do with its making it to shore. But in honesty, their bodies were worn and their minds were saturated, first with fear and then with relief.

The fog can do funny things to sailors in distress. When you're still and listening, you can hear the shoreline, hear the water break when it's near. But with the puttering of the engine and the splashing of the bailing buckets, there's no way to determine if the shore is a mile or a yard away. The fog can leave seafarers hopeless, but sometimes it can do the opposite: allow for one more turning of the bucket, one more sculling of the oars, just in case land is hiding behind the grey. By the time the three men had heard Oliver calling out, they were already exhausted and on the cusp of delirium. It would have been easy for Oliver Brown to have seemed like salvation, appearing through the fog.

As the story goes, Oliver met the boat with one hand gripping the keel and the other gripping the front edge of the bow. He had closed his eyes and forced every ounce of his strength into getting the boat to shore. The progress was constant but slow. Step by step, the heavy thirty-footer was pulled up onto the shore. He didn't stop or look at the others when his feet hit dry land. He kept pulling. The worn, salt-coated edge of the hull cut into his hands, tore open the soft skin on his palms, but he kept going, one step at a time. The wood of the hull creaked as it came up, higher and higher. His legs made high-arching steps as he moved between the logs. As he pulled the skiff from the water, the benefit of buoyancy was lost, and with each inch, it grew heavier. But this didn't stop him. Each step required all the strength he had, and the next one always required more. Oliver hauled the vessel, with water now pouring from the tear in its bottom, all the way up onto the shore.

The three fisherman who had manned the boat had long since stopped trying to help. They watched, soaking wet and exhausted, as a boy whose frame was slighter than half of any of theirs, performed a task that should have taken a dozen men—or so they'd say. It's impossible to determine how heavy the boat truly was, filled with water like that, or to know for certain how little or how much the fisherman had helped. Perhaps the Acadia had driven the boat further towards the shore than any of the men had realized, or had managed a few more turns after it'd been completely submerged. It's impossible to know for certain how much forward momentum was left and exactly how much work Oliver had done. But what is known is that, in the end, the boat was safe and dry on the slipway.

As the story goes, the fishermen stood knee deep in the water, silent and staring at the spectacle, backdropped by the fog. If that were true, Oliver wouldn't even have known, for he sat with his head hanging between his knees and his eyes closed. He was breathing so hard he was on the cusp of vomiting. His arms shook, his back spasmed.

When he realized there was a standing silence, Oliver managed to splutter, "What have ya done?"

None of the three men responded immediately, but his question stirred them to trudge up towards the shore. Clyde reached Oliver first. He put his hands under the young man's arms and effortlessly pulled him to standing.

Barry spoke slowly, methodically. "Struck a shoal," he said, "off Gull Rock. I cut it too close in the fog. I never seen how low the tide was." He looked back and forth over the length of his boat. Water still trickled out of the indented crack between two planks of the hull.

Oliver looked at each of the men after Clyde propped him up on his wobbling legs. He noticed their eyes were all on him and realized that perhaps they hadn't anticipated such success. His cheeks flushed further, embarrassment replacing the red of exertion. He tried to raise his chin; he pressed his shoulders back. Although he had filled out in recent years and his body was solid, he wasn't large. He had long wanted to prove to the fisherman of the town that he could manage the heavy work despite his frame, but now he just wanted to appear as large as possible. He no longer wanted them to believe he was strong, but instead, wanted them to believe that his strength was reasonable.

"Sorry 'bout your clothes," Clyde said.

Oliver looked down. He'd been wearing his Sunday slacks, usually reserved for church, and the best button-up shirt he owned. Despite not attending the funeral, he'd wanted to look respectable for when his aunt returned. But now he was soaked and salted. Mud and kelp clung to his ankles, and there was a tear up the back of his pant leg.

The church bells were no longer ringing. The fishing boat had almost stopped pouring water from its starboard side.

"It's alright," Oliver said, hardly loud enough for anyone to hear. He looked back and forth between the men. He was looking for an expression that offered comfort, even understanding, at least acceptance, but there was only uncertainty and disbelief.

Barry and Clyde had both been there, all those years ago, when Oliver and Johnathan had gone under the ice. It was the first time either of them had thought of that day in many years. They needn't say to one another that their minds had wandered there now because it was clear from their expressions. They'd never had cause to doubt their eyes or question their perception like that again, until now.

"I best be gettin' back," Oliver said. And with a wipe of his hands across the bottoms of his trousers, he began walking away.

He was thankful then for the thickness of the fog because he was gone from their sight in only a few strides. As soon as he knew they couldn't see him, Oliver ran. He sprinted back towards his aunt and uncle's house. He wasn't sure why he raced away from them. Nor why he didn't turn back when he heard Barry's voice, muffled in the mist. But he didn't want to be there any longer. He didn't like the way they looked at him. They didn't look at him as they did each other. They looked at him as if he was something different, something they didn't understand.

Bedlamer

A seal that has almost reached breeding age.

Four years before Oliver helped the Newports save their skiff, he had sat atop the northwest headland that guarded Salvage Harbour. Now he was fifteen—old enough to separate fairy tale and memory, but not yet old enough to know humanity's "motive for metaphor." The path to the top was a long and tedious trek from the nearest house, and it was on the far side of the harbour from Oliver's aunt and uncle's house. The path took him further inland than he liked. Most of it felt more like walking into the forest than venturing towards the coast. But that was the only manageable path up the hill there was. Despite the steep slope and the challenging journey, Oliver always found the destination worth it. Now he was a young teenager, and his legs had grown stronger, but he still felt uneasy when the path pulled him out of sight of the ocean. What was only a rounded hill from the land was a fearsome wall from the water.

Oliver could still remember the first time he saw that headland from a boat, coming back into the harbour. When he was a youngster, long before he was old enough to have walked to the spot where he now sat, Aubrey had taken Oliver and Aunt

Elizabeth out along the far shore to a place where a particularly hearty patch of gooseberries was growing. Oliver had been too young and too new to the open water to take in his surroundings as they'd made their way out of the harbour. His attention had been so consumed by the depth of the water over the side of the boat and the vastness of the sea in front of them that he hadn't bothered to look back. But when they'd left the far island shore for home again—with buckets and baskets filled with more berries than they could have hoped to collect—the menacing face of the cliff was inescapable. It was broad and jagged, and the top leaned out over the water as if unsupported by the base. It was so high that it made Oliver feel dizzy. The grandiose sight of it put a sensation of awe into the deepest parts of him.

The land to the crest of the hill was steep but manageable from the town. But from the sea, it was a vertical drop—a hundred yards or more—to crashing water. There were few places along the coastline that Oliver hadn't visited. He'd found every vantage point over the water and every slipway to the shore. But he liked that one, not just because it was the highest, but also because it was the hardest to get to. From there, on a clear day, Oliver could make out the town of Bonavista, miles across the bay.

The morning fog hadn't yet lifted off the water. It dissipated slowly, letting the view grow clearer as the sun rose higher in the sky. Through the fog, well beyond Little Denier, Oliver spied a large white form. He thought at first that it was an iceberg, creeping its way across the bay with the currents and tides. From April to late June, the waterways that cross in front of Salvage were littered with chunks of ice—some the size of houses, some churches, some towering as high as the headland that Oliver sat upon. He was told that they came from the north, from places that were more ice than land and that had always been that way.

Oliver tried to imagine what that would be like but had never ventured more than a few miles from his home. He had seen some neighbouring towns, but they were built on grounds almost identical to those beneath Salvage. They were the same towns in different places. As much as he'd heard of the vastness of the world, it was a size as incomprehensible as the stars beyond the sky to him.

The white shape that Oliver had spotted grew larger quickly. It moved with an intention that doesn't exist within ancient ice. Oliver watched for almost an hour as it grew closer and the fog grew thinner. Eventually, the consistent shape of the white angles and the dark green beneath them revealed the nature of the object. Under full dress, a schooner was on its way towards him, every sail opened to its fullest, taut and filled with wind. The schooner leaned on its side as it approached, the force of the full sails pulling it down as it was thrown forward. Even from a distance, Oliver could see how smoothly its keel cut the water. The constant swell that rolls on the outer seas forms steeper peaks as the ocean floor slowly rises to meet the land. Oliver watched the great boat break free from the crest of a swell for a moment, the speed of its approach launching the bow before the ocean sucked it back down, seamlessly returning to the water's surface. The boat belonged on the sea. Although every vessel is constructed to float, only a handful seem to be designed by the water itself. Only occasionally is a boat built as if its place atop the water is as much a birthright as a matter of buoyancy.

Oliver knew that schooner. It was the *Crystal Stream*, the Hunter family's boat, on its way into Salvage. He kept his eyes on the schooner for another few leagues, watching with admiration. Its sails shifted and it leaned to the other side, cutting tight between shoals and islands with perfect grace. Oliver tore himself from the sight and turned away from the sea to race back down the long path towards the harbour. The *Crystal Stream* had been moving goods from one port to another along the shore and hadn't taken port in Salvage in some months. After so long away, there was no doubt that it had been further than Greenspond and Bonavista. It must have been to St. John's and back, at least. Oliver was thrilled by the thought of this, by all the things that could possibly be in its holds. There could be fresh fruits or strange spices, perhaps even candy that'd be sold in the corner store.

While a few years ago he may have bounded his way down a steep hillside, as he grew older, he had gained caution and lost childish confidence. He wasn't as sure of his footing and was more sure of the repercussions of a fall. Oliver tried his best to rush down from the lookout, but the deeper he made his way into the thickness of the trees, the harder it became to find even footing. Sooner than later, his run had slowed to a hurried walk.

By the time Oliver descended the hillside, the *Crystal Stream* was already weaving its way into the harbour. The wharf where it would dock was at the other end of Bishop's Harbour, closer to Oliver's aunt and uncle's house, a distance that now seemed infinite. He knew that a crowd would have already gathered to watch the boat dock by the time he could get there, and his spirits dropped as he looked across the water, imagining the throng of people assembled to see what foreign items the boat brought with it. He'd have no chance of even glimpsing what the Hunter boys unloaded.

Free of the thickness of inland trees, Oliver had Salvage Harbour in front of him and the open bay behind him. He looked at the open water and the islands inhabited only by sheep and the blueberries that the sheep's grazing missed, away from where the schooner would soon be throwing lines. The sun had burned off the fog entirely, and the light hit the water's surface with constantly shifting shimmering. Every ripple of every wave caught light on its edges and textured the water.

As Oliver watched the moving light, he spotted a peculiar patch on the water, a dark place that didn't catch any light. While he'd matured in recent years, his curiosity hadn't decayed. His fondness for the ocean had only been fortified. He studied the patch of dark in the water, trying to see if the light would eventually reflect upon it the way that it did everywhere else, but the patch maintained a consistent darkness.

Although a small mystery in the ocean wasn't as compelling to Oliver as the schooner, avoiding being amidst the majority of the town was enough to guide him towards the water instead. But he couldn't approach the strange spot directly. He had to get to the shore first, past boulders and through bog patches. He tried to continually glance up and keep his eye on the peculiar place in the water, but waiting for it to reveal itself amongst the moving light and waves took too long at each stop. By the time he was on the rocky beach, he'd lost sight of it. He stood scanning the water for quite some time before realizing that what he was looking for wasn't part of the water but something floating upon it. Whatever it was had moved closer to shore by the time Oliver found it again, and it had moved further down the bay. He began walking along the coast, eyes trained on the mysterious object, leaving his home further behind.

The object continued drifting, constantly pulling him further away from the nearest house. Eventually, Oliver stopped chasing the strange sight. He accepted that he was chasing driftwood, and the further it took him away, the longer his walk home would be.

Oliver realized then, as he glanced back towards the water, that the object he had been pursuing had stopped drifting away from him. It had stopped when he had, and he thought for a moment that it seemed even closer, only ten yards from shore. This ignited his curiosity once more. Driftwood was influenced only by the currents and the waves, and Oliver couldn't think of anything that would interrupt either of those forces out where the driftwood seemed to have stopped.

He continued walking down the shore, noticing that as he did, the object was once again moving further away. Without another thought, Oliver began sprinting down the shore. The rocks gave way to a pebbled beach, which let his run garner more and more speed. He didn't bother looking at the floating thing he pursued, but just focussed on getting as far down the shore as possible.

Oliver ran until his heart pounded at his chest, and when he finally stopped, he immediately looked out at the water. Perfectly parallel to him, the object floated in the water, even closer. Still catching his breath, Oliver began walking again, and the moment he began moving forward, so did the object. When Oliver stopped again, the object—the creature—grew larger, rising out of the water.

"What are you?" Oliver said quietly. It looked almost like a person, dark hair matted to its head by salt water and eyes peeping above the surface. "Hey," he called to the creature. "What are you!"

To his surprise and delight, the creature seemed to respond. It immediately disappeared beneath the surface of the water, and each of its flippers and then its tail flicked up between the waves before its head emerged once more. It was almost as if the creature was showing off its appendages to confirm its identity. For a moment, Oliver pondered whether it could have been an otter or a mink, dramatically oversized. But despite an absence of familiarity, he recognized that it was a seal, its head bobbing up and down with the rolling of the waves. Oliver didn't know how to react so just continued looking at the animal, basking in his curiosity. The silent staring contest was broken when the seal flipped itself around and showed off its flippers once more, as if repeating its response to ensure that Oliver understood.

There was something different about the seal that Oliver couldn't quite place. Its nose seemed sharper, less like a muzzle and more like a face. Its big brown eyes met his, and they held one another's gaze.

Oliver began walking along the shore again, and the creature moved with him, swimming along in the water as he walked along the shore. It swam slowly closer to the beach as they proceeded.

"Well, you're a different kind of seal," Oliver said.

The creature dipped beneath the surface and then appeared again.

Oliver hadn't seen many seals in his lifetime. Few people sealed out of Salvage, and he never managed to see those who did bring in their catch. On occasion, a seal would come into the harbour on the sea ice, but it always seemed to be at a time when he wasn't allowed out because of too many chores or because his aunt said the weather was too poor.

He had no idea that there was a friendliness to the animals. That they might be just as interested in him as he was in them.

"Hello," he called, "my name is Oliver."

The seal tipped to its side and raised one flipper out of the water. As if it was waving to him.

This made Oliver smile. "Its nice to meet you" he said.

Then the creature disappeared.

Oliver stopped walking and scanned the water, trying to see where his new friend had gone. Just as he was becoming disappointed at the abrupt ending to the interaction, the seal appeared again, only a few yards away from him.

This was the first time that Oliver had gotten to see a seal so close, the first time he could see that its eyes were round and warm.

"You're quite pretty," he said.

The seal swam in a playful circle before facing Oliver once more. It tipped onto its back, briefly showing its belly, and then raised a flipper before swimming a little further out into the ocean. Oliver thought at first that his interaction with the creature had ended, but then it swam towards him once more and flipped onto its back, raising a flipper as if beckoning him into the water with it.

Oliver looked up and down the beach. It was a long way back to Salvage, but he could see a house further down the shore in the other direction and could just make out the flakes drying fish around the home. Surely, he thought, the house was too far away for anyone at home to be able to see him.

Oliver sat down on the rocks and began unlacing his boots.

The seal rose higher out of the water then, exposing its torso as it strained to get a view of what Oliver was doing.

"I'm coming," Oliver said. "But I can't get my clothes wet or Aunt Eliza will be mad somethin' terrible."

He had just stuffed his socks into his boots and stood to undo his belt when a deep voice came from behind him.

"You shouldn't be talkin' to seals."

Despite being gentle, the voice was so unexpected it made Oliver jump. He spun around to see Martin Ryan, standing just up on the bank with a cigarette hanging from his lips.

Martin didn't come any closer to Oliver. He just stood watching him with his hands in his pockets.

"You shouldn't go swimming with 'em either, son."

Fear flushed over Oliver. "I wasn't going to," he said. Searching for an explanation as to why he would be standing barefoot on the rocks.

"Aigh, knows you weren't either." Martin closed his lips, sucking on his cigarette and blowing the smoke out through his nose.

He turned and began walking away, towards the house that Oliver had seen down the shore.

Oliver scrambled to put his socks back onto his feet. "Wait!"

But as if deaf to his voice, Martin continued walking.

With boots back on, Oliver ran to catch up to the man. "Wait, Mr. Ryan!"

Martin continued walking as if he didn't hear him.

"Sir, please don't tell my aunt and uncle that I was gonna go swimmin', plea—"

"I told ye, son, long time back . . ." Martin turned his head so that the boy could hear him, but he didn't stop, or even look back. "It'd be more trouble for me to see ye swimming than ye being caught could ever cause."

Oliver stopped trying to follow him for a moment, considering the meaning of this statement, and then raced to catch up once more. "So you mean that you won't stop me from swimming?"

Oliver could see Martin shaking his head from behind.

"You shouldn't be talking to seals," he called back.

Oliver took double steps to try to catch up. "But why not?" he said.

Martin didn't say anything; he only continued walking. They were walking between wire grates of flaked fish now. The white fish was salted and left in the sun for the moisture to be sucked out, letting the cod last for many more months.

They were almost at the house on the beach. Beyond the home, Oliver could see the large shed with piles of long logs on one side of it and square-edged, bright yellow slabs on the other. Martin's small lumber mill.

Oliver tried to explain. "The seal talks back."

Martin shot the boy a look over his shoulder.

"Well, kinda. It was doin' tricks in the water when I talked to it."

Oliver stopped and looked back towards the harbour, seeing the tops of the masts of the *Crystal Stream* rising above the headland. Martin, almost at the door, stopped and turned towards him.

"You shouldn't be down here, son," he said. "Not by yourself. It's no good for either of us." He wore a pained expression but spoke with a harsher tone than Oliver had ever heard him use.

Oliver looked at his feet, not sure what to say. He hadn't considered that he could be making the man uncomfortable. He didn't understand what had caused that tone.

Martin sighed and spoke again. "It's not your fault, son. It's not mine either, but it took a long while to realize that." He rubbed the scruff on his chin and inhaled sharply. "Truth doesn't have much to do with how things are. It's about what people choose to believe. That's all that makes anything how anything is."

Oliver had heard of why Martin lived so far down the beach. It was the kind of story that's only told in bits and pieces unless someone was attempting to make it dramatic.

Martin had lived in Salvage once, the same as everyone else. Oliver didn't know which house had been his, or how long he'd lived there. Those kinds of things didn't seem worthy of retelling. Details that could be confirmed, or proven false, seem to disappear from stories over time. Most of what endures is at the mercy of imagination as much as reality.

Oliver had heard his aunt Liza say, with the plucking of a sharp tongue, "That Martin had a very close friend in his neighbour."

The word "friend" was always weighted in a way Oliver struggled to understand in his youth.

Depending on the storyteller—and the listener—the depths and repercussions of that friendship varied greatly. It seemed consistent that the neighbour was a married man, but not a single story included who the man was. In some stories, you'd hardly know the neighbour was married. His spouse could just as easily be mistaken for his sibling, they'd say. In other stories, the married couple were deeply in love until the moment that Martin moved in next door.

It's hard to know what led Martin to leave the town to build his sawmill on the beach. Some claim that the minister was called because it was a matter of ungodliness. Others say that it was the neighbour's wife, armed with a broom, who battered Martin and shooed him down the shore. Or perhaps no variation of these options was true, and the place on the beach was simply a good place to saw wood. The only thing irrefutable is that Martin had lived on his own, down the shore, ever since.

Oliver took a step back from Martin. It wasn't a move based in fear, or in uncertainty. It was an effort to be considerate. But despite Oliver's intentions, a certain sadness came across Martin's face when the boy distanced himself.

"It's best you get home," Martin said. "But you shouldn't be worried 'round me, son. I've never given a soul—God's sake a child—any hint of a reason to be afraid around me . . . At least no reason true."

"I'm not afraid," Oliver said.

Martin sighed once more. "Go on home, son. And don't go talkin' to seals."

Oliver clasped his hands in front of himself, fingers intertwined and squeezed tight. He turned as if to walk away but then waited a long moment. He turned back and spoke louder than he'd intended to. "Is it because of my mother?"

Martin and Oliver met one another's eyes. Martin held the gaze long and hard before sighing deeply and looking away. He reached for the window ledge of his home, where a pouch of tobacco sat, and pulled out a limp cigarette, already rolled. Oliver hadn't even noticed him finish the first one. Martin was looking out towards the water now, where the seal still bobbed up and down.

"No, lad," Martin said. "I was always told, ye never speak to the seals."

Oliver clenched his hands in frustration. "But why not?"

"Well"—Martin paused to light his cigarette—"because they'll talk back."

Oliver hesitated. "Well, it didn't really say anything."

"But it knew you were saying something. Something kind. And it listened."

"I like that, though," Oliver said, kicking gently at the beach stones under his feet.

"Aigh, and so will any sealer in town."

Oliver was silent then.

"It makes 'em comfortable. If ye talk to the seals, they'll come looking for conversation. They'll listen to any ol' person. And not all people wish 'em well."

"Is that how the sealers get them?" Oliver said.

"Nay, son, not the ones I know," Martin said, taking a long drag on his cigarette. "There's something particularly cruel about using friendship to kill something. Most sealers are good enough with a gun and a stick that they don't need to tease the animal first."

"Oh," Oliver said.

The seal looked at the pair as it floated in the water, its big brown eyes bobbing just above the surface.

"Doesn't it not make a difference then? If I talk to them or not."

Martin chewed his lip and gave a shrug, "Aigh, lad. I s'pose ye could look at it that way. So long as ye don't mind knowin' that yer friendship might make the creature's life shorter."

There was a long silence then. Neither of them was sure of quite what to say.

"Perhaps it's not my place to tell ye not to talk to 'em," Martin said, eyes still on the seal as it bobbed up and down. "I'm no stranger to loneliness, and I gather you're getting to know it well, too. Maybe I shouldn't keep ye from the water at all."

Oliver took his turn to sigh. "I wouldn't want it to get hurt just because I was trying to make it my friend." He had already learned that his company could be dangerous for others.

"Aigh. And I wouldn't want ye endin' up hurt because anyone learned ye kept friends with a seal."

Oliver looked at Martin, maintaining the silence for too long. "It's because of my mother," he said.

Martin wet his thumb and forefinger with his tongue and pinched the ember at the end of his cigarette. He put the douted cigarette in his breast pocket and opened the door to his house. "It's only to do with the stories that are told, lad."

Martin went inside and closed the door tight behind him, leaving Oliver standing alone on the beach. The seal had long since disappeared back into the ocean.

Yarn

An often fictitious story that is told orally and repeated by various storytellers regardless of proximity to source.

Oliver sat at the tip of the point that extended into the middle of Bishop's Harbour, his shirt undone to let the cool air try to find his skin. It had been nearly six years since the day on the ice pans, and he would be seventeen in a few months. While his frame was still slight, his shoulders had grown broader, and the muscles of adulthood had begun to appear across his chest and arms. The lights of fires, scattered across the town, floated as broken reflections upon the water, but he was looking without seeing, his mind in places his eyes couldn't reach. It was the fifth of November, Bonfire Night, and one fire—a communal pile of scrap wood from everyone in town, with a fisherman scarecrow acting as an effigy on the top—burned brightest for the town to enjoy. Many folks burned what they could near their own homes. Stalks from the last potato harvest and remnants of retired boats and fences all up in flames on this night to recognize a mostly forgotten tradition. People gathered around all these fires, but Oliver couldn't bring himself to stand near the heat of any of them, even if he had been invited.

He looked across the water to a place he couldn't see and couldn't know. He looked for a place where being alone wouldn't feel quite as lonely, where being on his own would be a choice and not an obligation of circumstance. But a place where he could be in harmony with other people seemed too much to even fantasize about, and so he dreamt only of a place where he could be at peace.

As he sat, looking without seeing, he heard a gentle change in the water. It was the slightest shift, almost imperceptible, but Oliver knew the ocean better than most fishermen knew their gunwales. He heard the waves begin to hesitate before they lapped against the rocks and felt the momentum of the water pulling away instead of pushing forward. The tide was turning. The ocean was beginning to drag itself back from the shore.

At first Oliver paid little attention to the shifting of the tides, but as the ocean moved with the invisible force of an unseen new moon, it pulled more than water back with it. The sounds on the shore stuck to the waves and were towed out into the bay. While before there had been silence, the departure of the water now revealed the sounds of Oliver's peers somewhere behind him along the beach. The voices that the tides carried were familiar, but he didn't look towards them. He knew where the teenagers would be, tucked into the elbow of the beach and the point, out of view of the houses further up the hill, and hidden from his view by the fractured skeleton of the rocky finger he sat on the tip of. The group was a hundred yards closer to shore than Oliver, but the still night and dropping tide brought their voices closer and closer.

The crackling sounds of their bonfire grew clearer, and soon he could hear every word that was said and identify each of the voices. He assumed there were others but could distinctly make out at least four members of the group. Clayton Saunders, his words squeaking with his usual excitement. Gary Matchim, crass and grumbly. Rosie Ryan, sharp tongued and confident. And Johnathan Genge. Even though it had changed since their youth, Oliver could always recognize Johnathan's voice. He heard it differently from the others, in his gut instead of his ears.

There was chatter over sharing stolen drinks and stoking the fire. A complaint about the cold, and then a complaint about an empty bottle. Some of the youths' interactions seemed foreign to Oliver. They spoke to each other in ways he had never experienced and had stopped trying to understand. He didn't focus on what they said until he heard an exclamation.

"Did ya see that!" Clayton Saunders' voice was deeper than it had been years ago when he'd yelled about Oliver on the ice pans, but it still had a shrillness to it.

"See what?" Gary Matchim asked.

"A light, out there, in the cove."

"Go on wi'cha," Johnathan Genge said. "There's nar thing out there."

"No, b'ys, I swear. A light was right out there, off the point."

There had been no light. Oliver had been absorbing the darkness for a long while, and nothing had broken it. Whatever had caught Clayton's attention had come from the fire, not the sea.

"Sure, what would the light be from, Clayt?" Rosie Ryan spoke with a sarcastic tone.

"Listen, I tells ya I saw it."

"There's stories about lights off the points." Oliver recognized Rebecca Smith's voice. He wondered if she sat next to Johnathan, if he held her close, if he kept her warm. Oliver had noticed the increase in their intimacy in the last couple of months—the way they looked at each other, the way they always sat together.

"Oh, yes, yes! Tell us a story, Becky." Rosie's voice bubbled with excitement.

Johnathan encouraged his girlfriend. "Go on then."

"Well, listen. This one's not about that point. Not even this harbour. I heard it from my grandmother Collins down in Eastport."

There was a pause then. Oliver could hear only the crackling of the fire and imagined that Rebecca was drinking from a bottle of something that they weren't supposed to have. He imagined she was making the others wait on purpose to make the story more dramatic.

"See, years ago, an old feller used to live out on the point by Eastport Beach. He always lived alone, would only come into town once or twice a year to buy a bit of oil for his lamp. Anyway, no one really knew him, but they all knew of him. And every night, the minute it struck midnight, you'd see a lamp come on in one of his windows."

"Awful late to light a lamp," Clayton said.

"Who'd be awake to even see it, sure."

"Well, it happened every night, see," Rebecca explained. "So over the years, everyone saw it now and again. And apparently it came on at the exact same time: you could set your watch to it, they said. But then one night, someone noticed that there was no light out on the point. No one thought too much of it. They just found it a bit peculiar. But a few weeks passed, and there was nar light. So finally, someone said that they best go check on the old feller, and sure enough, when they gets out there, he was ready for the ground. Like, long dead. So dead they could smell 'im before they gets the door open."

Gary huffed. "Oh I 'llows now."

Rebecca continued. "That's what they says! Apparently, the smell was so bad they couldn't get it out of the house. It was stuck in it, soaked right up into the wood. So after buddy is buried and gone, b'ys in the town decided the only thing that could be done was to burn the house down so that—one day—someone could build a house out there again."

"Burned a house down 'cause of a smell!" Clayton said. "Yes b'y, some kind of waste."

"Well, he had no children, no family or nothin', and no one wanted to take the time to clean it, so that's what they did," Rebecca explained. "Anyway, the old man is in the ground, and nothing's left of the house but the bare spot from the end of the trail to the shore. But a few weeks later, someone walking home sees a light out on the point. They don't think nothin' of it. But the next night, it's out there again. The minute that it gets to midnight, there's a light out on the—"

"So someone was going out on the point!" Gary said, and then there was the sudden, sharp sound of glass against rocks just a few feet behind Oliver.

His heart jumped. Gary must had thrown his beer bottle to underline his point, and for a moment, the voices of the group around the fire were drowned out by the cascading shards of glass finding new homes in the crevices of the point.

"Well, that's exactly what they all thought," Gary said. "And this goes on for weeks and weeks, right? But then someone buys the land! They were gonna build out on it, but they figures they got someone trespassing out there every night. So the person who bought it goes out there one night, and he waits and waits, and midnight comes and goes, but there's no one to be seen. So the next morning he's telling this story, sayin' he must have scared off whoever it was. But everyone in the town says that they'd seen the light the night before! Now buddy, the new landlord, says that's not possible 'tall. He was out there all night, he didn't see a soul, and he didn't see nar light. But the folks in the town are adamant that it was out there. So the next night, the feller waits on the beach until midnight, and sure enough, a light appears. He heads straight out there, all ready to have a scuff. But when he gets to the point, no one's to be seen. No person, not even a sign that a person had been there. Just a light. Just one bright light floating in the air."

"Whadda ya mean, floating?" Clayton said, poorly hiding the alarm in his voice.

"What I said. It's just there off the ground, a light attached to nothing."

"Wha', like a lamp?"

"I don't know, like a light." Rebecca sounded exasperated.

"Like a ball of light?"

"Clayt, it was a light, b'y. Let her tell the story," Johnathan said, garnering chuckles from the group.

"Well, he sees the light," Rebecca continued. "And now everyone in the town knew he was out there waiting that night, so they're all watching. And they say that, all of a sudden, the light moved from where it was and shot right in across the shore and disappeared. So they didn't think too much of it—"

"Didn't think much of it?" Clayton said. "Sure seems like they should have."

"Yeah, the crowd down Eastport right used to ghosts or wha'?" Gary added.

"Well," Rebecca said, "they didn't know what to think of it—"

"Flying lights," Gary said. "I s'pose they didn't—"

"Just let her keep telling the story!" Rosie's voice came louder than usual to cut through the bickering.

"Yes, yes. It was strange!" Rebecca said. "I don't know what they thought of it . . . But as the story goes, the next day, the feller who bought the land is spotted in town packing up his truck. He doesn't talk to anyone, he doesn't say a word, he just leaves the town and never comes back. And to this day, not a soul has built out on that point. And they still says that, if you look close at midnight, you can see the light above the point."

"Hold on, now," Gary said.

Oliver could hear the groans and giggles from the others around the fire the moment that Gary began to speak.

"No, no, just hear me out! If he didn't talk to anyone, how do you know he saw the light floating?"

The group broke into a heated conversation over the amount of truth needed in the retelling of a story.

"Alright. Alright. I got one, b'ys," Johnathan said, cutting into the chaos and silencing the group.

Oliver wished he could turn around to try and make out Johnathan's face in the firelight. He wanted to see his expressions as he spoke. He wanted to see the animation on his face, a smile on his lips, and the brightness in his eyes. Oliver hadn't heard Johnathan say more than a sentence for years and missed his voice. Oliver realized that Johnathan's voice had changed and wasn't quite the same as when they were young. But nothing was.

"My fadder told me this one," Johnathan said.

"What, did it happen to him?" Gary already sounded skeptical.

"No. It was a buddy he had out on the boat with 'im for a while."

"Sure it was," Gary said.

"You're crooked as sin 'ere tonight, Matchim," Rosie snapped.

"It was an old guy that told Fadder. Buddy had been on the water his whole life—born wit' a fishing line in his hand, right?

So Fadder was fishing off the end of Swale Island, and it'd been a real slow day. Nudding all morning or afternoon 'til they got to that last spot. So fish starts coming in, and Fadder wants to keep on fishing so long as he can. But the sun's gettin' low in the sky, right? And this old feller who Dad has wit' him says that they need to go back in. Fadder tells him no, that he wants a few more fish first. And buddy says no, they gotta go in because he's seen sea monsters out there . . . Imagine that! Sea monsters."

The group was quiet for a moment before Rosie broke the silence. "Is that it?"

"Well, yeah. Buddy said he'd seen a sea monster."

"Johnny, you're some bad at tellin' stories," Clayton said.

Laughter came from the group.

An anger flared in Oliver. He almost jumped up to see who all had laughed at Johnathan. Even with his shirt undone, he felt the back of his neck grow hot as Johnathan was being mocked. But before Oliver was overwhelmed by a protective instinct, he discerned Johnathan's laugh amongst the others. The shared humour cooled him, and he reminded himself that he had come out to the point to look out across the black water, not to listen to the young townspeople behind him. Across the sea he hoped there was something that he couldn't find in Salvage.

"It's a good story, b'ys," Johnathan said. His voice was too easy to hear for the sea to drown it out, and despite himself, Oliver began listening again.

"It is," said Rebecca. "I heard his father tell it."

"Is that the ending then?" Rosie asked.

"Well, I wouldn't have ended it quite that way," Rebecca said. There was a sly teasing in her voice, and Oliver could imagine the smirk she would have worn. He didn't like that expression, even if it was just in his imagination.

"Go on, you tell it then," Johnathan said. "You're better at spinning a yarn."

"Yes, do it justice for Jesus's sake, Becky," Clayton said.

"Okay, okay."

Rosie squealed, clapped once and then added a quick series of claps.

"Well," Rebecca began, "the way I heard it is that when Johnathan's father, Clarke, first said he wanted to stay, the buddy in the boat with him didn't really say much at all. He hadn't been working for him long, right? So he didn't wanna get on his skipper's bad side. So buddy fishes away for another half hour and then just starts pulling in his line and folding in the net. So Clarke says to him, 'Buddy, what do you think you're doing? There's still work to be done.' And this feller just says that it's gettin' dark and they gotta go. So Clarke says, 'No, b'y, I knows the way home like the back of my hand. The seas are calm and the fish is good.' Now at first, Clarke thinks this is the end of it and goes back to work, but suddenly he hears the motor turn over and he realizes the whole damned boat is moving! Buddy had gone back to the tiller and just started pulling away. And here's Clarke with his net still in the water! So he storms to the back of the boat, full intentions of going up one side of this old feller and back down the other. But when he gets to the stern, this buddy has a gaff in his hand, and he holds it right up in front of him, level with Clarke's throat."

"Jesus Christ, what was buddy, nuts? Sure, I wouldn't have a go at your fadder if he was tied down and I had a shotgun," Gary said.

Oliver understood the young Matchim's point. Johnathan's father was a mountain of a man. He had witnessed his temper firsthand.

"Not nuts," Rebecca said. "Terrified. Clarke said he's never seen someone so scared in all his life. He's holdin' up the gaff, and he says to Clarke, 'I'm leaving this place one way or another.' He says he don't care if he's got to swim. He's not crossing the sound in the night."

"Johnny, how the hell did you leave all this out?" Gary said. "You really are shite at tellin' stories."

The young people all laughed at this.

Rebecca waited until silence had returned before she continued her story. "So, Clarke doesn't wanna get in a scuff with this old feller in the middle of the water, and he figures what few fish he'd catch in the next hour aren't quite worth drownin' a man. So he lets buddy start guiding the boat home. But on the jaunt back, Clarke says to him, 'Jesus, ol' man, what is there that can be seen that'd give you that kind of a fright?' And buddy says, 'The . . . squid!'"

"I knew it," Clayton shouted. "I knew it was gonna be 'bout the giant squid."

"This feller was convinced that years ago, a boat he was on got attacked by a squid. He says they was trying to get into Happy Adventure for the night. They were out on the water later than they were supposed to be, and suddenly, the skiff slams into something, like striking a shoal—but it's out in the middle of the sound where there's leagues of water and not a rock. But the boat just came up solid. So when they run to the bow to look over and see what it is, they see the whole water movin'. There's long slippery tentacles all through the water, twisting and turning around it, hundreds of feet long, slithering and coiling in every direction. They hear the wood start creakin' and then they hear a splinterin', and they realizes that the thing is crushing the whole goddamn boat. Someone grabs a rifle that's on board for shootin' turrs, and they starts pumpin' shots into the thing. The other b'ys go and grab everything they've got to start throwin' over the side. But the thing is so big it's as if it's takin' up the whole water, and no one knows what to try and hit and if it's gonna do anything 'tall. Anyway, one of the shots must have hurt or something, because the water suddenly got twice as black as it was before and the thing disappeared. They manage to limp the boat in, but she was leakin' from every crack and had to be dry-docked for a month. When they pulled her up, the whole base of her was dyed black. Completely soaked through with ink. So buddy was convinced it was because they were on the water after dark, and refuses to ever get caught out there again. He swears on the Bible and his own mudder's grave that there's a boat eater out in those waters."

Clayton jumped in the moment that Rebecca stopped speaking. "I believes it."

"Sure you does," Gary said.

"I does. There's weird things out there in that water."

Gary balked. "Giant squid is a load of foolishness."

"Foolish or not, I still thinks it's scary," Rosie admitted.

Johnathan spoke up. "There's better things than squid to be scared of out there."

"Like what?" Clayton said.

"Like the mermaids," Gary interjected.

Johnathan sighed. "Well, I meant gales."

"Mermaids," said Clayton. "You don't believe in the giant squid, Gary, but you thinks there's fish people."

"I didn't say I believe in them, but if there's anything to be scared of, it's the mermaids and the selkies. They're the people eaters."

Oliver shivered, Gary's words chilling him in a way the weather never could.

"People eaters?" Rosie's voice came in quiet.

"The lot of 'em," Gary said. "There isn't a fisherman who doesn't have a story about hearing a maiden singing out in the ocean, and the only reason they do it is to try and lure ya in to eat ya."

"Now that's foolishness," Johnathan said.

"You just says that because you owes one your life," said Gary.

"Bullshit." Johnathan's response was quick.

"What's that all about?" Rebecca asked.

"Oliver Brown," Gary said. "He's half-seal."

Rebecca pressed him. "What are you talkin' about?"

"Wha', don't tell me you haven't heard that?" Rosie said.

Oliver willed them to stop speaking. He didn't want to hear what they had to say about him. But their voices seemed to be all around him, and he couldn't escape them. He didn't want to leave the point and risk being seen, but there was no way to stop listening as he sat there.

"Remember all them years ago out on the ice, when Oliver and Johnathan went under?" Clayton asked Rebecca. "Didn't you ever wonder how come Johnny almost died but Oliver was best kind?"

"I don't know. Not really," she said.

Gary snorted. "It's 'cause his mudder was a seal."

"There's not a word of truth to that," Johnathan said.

"Listen, there's somethin' wrong with 'im."

Rosie piped in. "He is some weird."

"I mean, he might be a bit different, but that doesn't mean that his mother was a seal," Rebecca said.

"She came right out of the ocean. That's one thing I believes," Gary said. "See, there wasn't a soul in town who knew her, but one day she just showed up here. She's young and right pretty, and she's lookin' for a man. She could have laid down with half the men in town and convinced any one of 'em to marry her. But it was poor old Albert Brown that she set her sights on. They're conniving creatures, right? They've got a way of blinding their lovers so they can't see nudding else. Every night, she'd go down to the water, put on a sealskin, and leave town. I'm sure she had a seal husband and pups and the whole thing, but that wasn't good enough. She wanted the human one too. And everyone told Albert there was somethin' not right with her. They told him that she was trouble. But he couldn't be reasoned with. He was right bewitched by her beauty. So she gets pregnant right away, and not even three months later, she has a babe."

"That's not true," said Rosie, clicking her tongue.

"It is too." Gary laughed. "Just like a seal, she don't need to carry the baby so long. Gets pregnant in the winter and has the pups in the spring."

"Seals are pregnant for ages, longer than people." Rebecca returned the same type of criticism Gary had thrown at her. "If you stopped carving your desk long 'nough to look at a teacher, you might know that. Wives' tales," she said definitively.

"Yes, and lights out on the points ain't?" said Clayton.

Rosie piped in again, her voice still quiet. "I dunno. He's strange, but he doesn't look like a seal."

"Not now, but that's only because the doc had to fix him." Gary spoke with such confidence that it made Oliver's stomach churn. "He was born with his legs stuck together—all flat footed like it was one tail—and webbed fingers and toes 'cause he's not meant to be on the land with the likes of us."

"Where'd you hear that too 'tall, Gary," Rebecca said.

"Sure, it was the talk of the town back then."

"Back when you were still in a crib yerself."

"I don't know where you heard it to," Johnathan said, "but not a word of it's true."

"I swear to Jesus," said Gary, "if you ever look at his hands, in between the fingers is all scars from where they had to cut 'em apart and take off all the webbing."

"That's true," said Clayton, "I've seen his fingers with my own eyes."

In the dark at the end of the point, Oliver found himself looking at his own hands. He knew that he had no scars. He knew that he hadn't been born in the way that Gary Matchim had described. He knew that he hadn't had webbed feet or hands. But the boy's assertiveness made him question his own body. Oliver knew that Johnathan knew the difference. He had held Oliver's hands on enough occasions that he knew there were no scars. But Johnathan didn't say anything more about that truth.

"Soon as Albert got the doc to turn 'im back into something more like a person, Oliver's mum probably would have ate 'im!" Gary said. "If Albert wasn't still around."

"Well, why didn't she when Albert got taken away on the boat with the consumption?" Johnathan said.

"Because by then," Gary said, "she'd already started teaching that boy her ways. She wanted him to grow up to be like her, to take him back to the ocean to be a seal person with her. She just never got to."

"Well, what happened to her?"

"With no man around, she wants to find another mate then, to have more pups to take out to sea with her, or to eat and keep her and Oliver fed, right? But, selkies age the same as seals, see. So she was right beautiful when Albert married her, but in a couple years, she was an old hag, gotten right fat with big long whiskers, just like a seal. She couldn't use her looks to get none of the men in town, so instead, she started singing. And to all the men in town it sounded like the most beautiful thing they've ever heard. But to the women, it sounded like wailing and screeching. So she starts singing every night, luring all the men in town up to her, right?"

"This sounds like a different story," Rebecca said.

"It's not," Gary said. "This is what happened."

"I thought sirens were the ones that sang." Rebecca said.

"It's all the same—"

"Just finish the story!" Clayton demanded.

Oliver's stomach twisted. He hated the story that was being told and knew there was no truth to it. He knew that it was all ridiculous, as unreal as the story of a floating light above the point and the giant, boat-crushing squid. It was as make-believe as the fairies in the woods that would steal crumbs from children's pockets. But it doesn't take something to be real for it to hurt. Every word Gary spoke about Oliver's mother, about Oliver, tore through something inside him that was usually too deep to be touched. Like the keel of a schooner running aground in a virgin cove, the story carved a gash in him that would last far longer than the boat. Oliver held his arms over his head, hoping to muffle their words.

Gary continued. "So she lives in the house with Oliver, and now she never needs to leave the house because the men came up every night and give her what she wants. And then she has the babies that she can eat. So she just stays up there, getting fatter and grosser and collecting seal pups to take back to the ocean with her—"

A splash came from the harbour, and Gary's story was cut short. All the group turned and looked towards the blackness of the sea. The sound wasn't loud, but the night was calm and quiet, and the breaking of the gentle lapping of water against the shore stood out. The noise tore them all away from their fire and from each other's company. Stoked with fear from the stories they had told each other, their perception tainted by the exercising of their imaginations, the youths were all convinced—independently and collectively—that something sinister had just slipped into the water.

There was no way for them to have known that the sound they'd heard was Oliver diving from the point. There was no reason for any of them to suspect that Oliver had been hidden out there in the darkness at all. But they all shuffled uncomfortably, moving closer to the fire and pretending not to be watching the water from the corners of their eyes.

Rebecca would come to say that Johnathan hadn't budged in his seat. After hearing the sound, he had sat perfectly still and looked at the harbour mouth, scanning the water. Johnathan's eyes hadn't been wide with fear, but the corners of his mouth had been pulled down with concern. He didn't join in with the others as they joked about what the sound could have been to hide their fear. He just looked out across the water with a sadness that wasn't all his own.

Gone

Someone who has lost their mental capacity or their understanding of reality.

The saving of the Newports' skiff was some four years after Oliver's encounter with a grey seal near Martin Ryan's house. After leaving the men at the wharf, seventeen-year-old Oliver neared his aunt and uncle's home and slowed from his sprint. He had run the entire distance from the wharf, not slowing once since leaving the Newports staring after him in the fog. With shuffling steps and dragging heels, he caught his breath for the last few yards.

Aubrey was sitting on the stoop of the back door. Oliver couldn't see the house until he was almost upon it, let alone make out the form of his uncle. Aubrey heard him approaching, though. "Thick as pea soup," he said, speaking through the fog.

Oliver was trying to slow his breathing and didn't say anything. His heart was battering his ribcage; he could feel it through his chest. His whole body shivered, and he could feel the blood in his veins as it pumped with the beat of his heart.

Almost on the stoop, he crept forward slowly, looking at the ground like a dog with its tail between its legs, awaiting a reprimand.

"Jesus, my son. What's the state of ya?" Aubrey stood up. His black tie hung undone around his neck.

Oliver's breathing was almost even, but he wasn't sure how to summarize the last half an hour into a simple answer. "Newport's skiff," he said, "struck a shoal."

Aubrey stared at the boy. His eyes had moved from muddy trousers and untucked shirt to Oliver's face. His mouth opened and then closed again. It was clear he wanted to ask what the Newport's boat had to do with Oliver. He wanted to ask how he'd been involved in their striking of a shoal. But more pressing concerns were on hand.

"Your aunt is on her way down from May's. You best get inside before she sees ya like this."

Oliver swallowed and began walking up the stairs to the door.

"Christ, b'y. Of all the days for you to come back in a state like that."

Oliver was opening the door.

"You're some lucky May told her to drop in for some tea."

Oliver's foot was on the threshold, a pace away from safety, when Elizabeth's voice cut through the fog.

"And what makes anybody lucky on a day like today?" she said, louder than was necessary, as her form appeared through the mist. May was on one side of her. Irene was on the other.

At that moment, Oliver still could have slipped inside. Chances are he could have walked into the house, run up the stairs, and been followed only by his aunt's shouted inquiries. He could have gotten away without her seeing the state of his best clothes. He would only have been reprimanded for being underdressed.

But Oliver stayed on the step. He turned back towards Elizabeth with his chin almost touching his chest. Perhaps he was tired from running. Perhaps he was tired from helping. Perhaps

Oliver was profoundly tired, too tired to put self-preservation before self-respect. Oliver stood before his aunt and her companions, and he lifted his head, meeting their gaze.

"Oh, my souls." Irene's voice was high and alarmed. "Look at the state of him."

"What 'ave ya got done?" May hissed.

Elizabeth didn't say anything, though. Oliver met her gaze, waiting for her reprimand. But nothing came. She stared at him with a blank expression.

There was a long pause. No one spoke, but Irene made quiet tutting sounds as she stared at Oliver.

"I'll go put on a change of clothes," he said.

"Why?" Elizabeth asked sharply. "Why are ya gonna go put on a change of clothes?"

Oliver hesitated then looked down at himself, coated in mud, with the white stains of salt water drying on black fabric.

"Sure, you didn't have enough respect to be sensible in the first place. Why are ya gonna go get changed?"

"I was dressed sensible, but—"

"You was, yeah. You was dressed in your best long enough to ruin your good clothes. Ruin good clothes I bought for ya. Dressed up just to insult me, just to be cruel to me."

"No, I—"

"That's just shameful," Irene said. "You're a disgrace. After all your aunt has done for you."

"I didn't mean to get in a state. I was trying to help the Newports."

"Of all the days for you to be causing trouble, Oliver Brown. Of all the days. I thought even you would be better than this today."

"I wasn't causing trouble."

"The day of your grandmudder's funeral. That's just shameful," May said, with a shake of her head.

Oliver looked at May. He clenched his teeth together.

"Was it?" He felt his cheeks flush the moment he said the words. His heart beat faster, but he kept his jaw locked, refusing to show his reservations.

"What did you say?" Irene said, with some genuine uncertainty.

"Was it my grandmother's funeral today? Was she my grandmother? I didn't know that." Oliver looked directly at Elizabeth as he spoke.

The extent of Oliver's meaning was lost on Irene and May. But Elizabeth knew. She knew that she'd never spoken aloud of their relation. She knew she'd never told the boy that he was related to the woman who'd lived down the hill. Elizabeth had only ever referred to the woman as her sister. She'd left Oliver to put it together on his own, without any concern for whether he did or not.

May pitched in, unaware of the staring contest between Oliver and Elizabeth. "Margret was your father's mother, boy. Don't pretend like you didn't know that."

"Just because she was my father's mother doesn't mean she was any grandmother to me."

"That's enough now," Aubrey said, louder than any of the others had been speaking. He stood up from his perch on the steps. He was slow to rise, not from intention but requirement. His knees were stiff these days. His bones creaked, years on the sea finally showing on his body.

"Whether you knew her or not, she was your grandmother, Oliver Brown. Same as you didn't know your father. You can't choose your blood," Elizabeth said. Her voice was unnervingly calm.

"My father didn't choose not to know me." Oliver ground his teeth.

"Your father would never've chosen to be so disrespectful to the woman that raised 'im either," Irene said.

Elizabeth straightened her back and pushed back her shoulders, staring down her nose at her nephew. "Aye, but your mother did."

"You're just like your mother. No respect," Irene spat.

"If blood could be chosen, you wouldn't 'ave chosen hers," May added.

Elizabeth nodded along with them, "And your mother's blood is why Margret kept her distance from you, and that's no more your fault than it is my sister's."

Oliver's hands were clenched so tight that his knuckles strained to break free of the skin. Blood was held tight against his palms, pooling in the folds of the soft skin the boat keel had torn apart.

"My mother hasn't got anything to do with it."

"Your mother has everything to do with it. I know you think you know so much. But you 'aven't a clue who she was, what she was." Elizabeth shook her head slowly. "I feel sorry for you, boy, needin' to be the offspring of her."

"I'm not ashamed of my mother." Oliver's voice was growing louder. He spit as he spoke.

"You ought to be," Elizabeth said. "She's the one you should blame for 'ow your life is. You might've been 'alf-normal if it wasn't for she."

"There's nothing wrong with being different. It's everyone else—"

"Luh, luh." Elizabeth jerked her chin with her words. "It's like Martin Ryan is speaking right off yer lips. You think that ol' pervert has got any clue."

"He's not a pervert. He's just—"

"Different. Yes, yeah!" Elizabeth's voice raised up sharp and fast, leaving spittle across her chin. She wiped her face and continued in a cold, flat tone. "He's different, alright, and he'll pay for his sins when the Lord comes. Do you actually believe those stories he told you?"

Oliver's face, already red with anger, flushed a shade darker as his eyes grew wide.

"Did you think I wasn't listening? Oh, I heard every word of it. I wasn't about to let that man be near a child without keeping watch—"

"He's never touched a child." Oliver's hands were clenched so tight his arms began to tremble.

"It don't matter. If he's so sick as to want other men, then there's nar thing beyond him." Elizabeth looked to the sky as if what she was declaring even God would agree with.

"That's not true—"

"Oh, and you knows do—"

"Elizabeth," Aubrey said, his voice coming in sharp.

Elizabeth looked at Aubrey, her nostrils flared. She exhaled and looked back at Oliver.

"I didn't think there was any harm in you hearing some old wives' tales, but I never for the life of me thought you'd believe 'em. But you do still, don't ya?" Elizabeth laughed then, a laugh forced out with shallow breaths. "You poor fool."

"He just told me what you all believed. At least he told me somethin'."

"Told ya what. What'd he tell you?" Elizabeth put her hand on her hip.

"My mother was different, and you all hated her for it." Oliver's words rasped as he tried to keep tears at bay. "It's your fault, your fault for hating her. That's why she's not here."

"Oh my souls," May shouted. She turned from the group and walked away, fanning her face with her hand. Irene followed after her, putting an arm over May's shoulder.

"Is that really what you think?" Elizabeth said.

Oliver kept his lips tight together. Irene and May had walked far enough away that the fog obscured them again.

"Is that really what you think?" she said again, her tone a little harder, demanding an answer.

"Elizabeth, that's enough." Aubrey said, but his voice wasn't as fierce as it had been. He didn't speak with the authority Oliver had heard so many times.

"You all hated my mother. She was alone, and she's still alone. You even buried her all alone."

"Your mother was evil, Oliver Brown."

"She wasn't."

Elizabeth leaned forward, as if shortening the distance between them would make the words hit him harder. "Your mother, whatever she was, was terrible. The only favour she ever did you was dying."

"That's not true. She loved me—"

"Loved you?" Elizabeth huffed. "You'd be dead if she hadn't left when she did. You wouldn't have lived long enough to defend her."

"That's not true." Oliver's voice cracked into a squeak on the last syllable.

"You don't know anything about truth. You weren't old enough to remember, and I thanked the Lord for that every day."

"Elizabeth!" Aubrey was shouting now.

Elizabeth shouted back. "Aubrey, why shouldn't the boy know? Why shouldn't he know what his mother was?"

"I know what you all think my mother was."

"No, no, you thinks she was some kind of a seal, don't ya? What nonsense. Stories, stories people made up to try and understand what they don't. Stories to make them feel better. Your mother was no creature from the sea, but she might as well have been a monster. She might as well've 'ad scales." Elizabeth exhaled long and hard. "I was there. I was there the first time."

"At the Legion?" Oliver's mouth was dry. Uncertainty softened the emotion in his tone.

"Wha'? When they met?" Elizabeth looked down and shook her head. "Oh, I was there too. And I didn't like her then. You could tell she wasn't right. The way she barely spoke. She had a look in her eye, like she hadn't a clue what anyone was saying to her, like her mind was always somewhere else. Sure, she showed up wearing Stella's dress, stolen right off the clothesline that afternoon. No, my son, for all I told Albert to keep clear of her at the Legion, that's not the first time that I'm talking about."

The frustration that had boiled Oliver's blood, the anger that had flushed his face, began to fade with a coming discovery. There was a space, a void in the story that Oliver had spent his entire life compiling without realizing that he was doing so. He had filled the space with the drippings of fuller stories, the cuttings of things he'd heard or thought to be true, and the believable parts of tellings he knew to be false. He knew, somehow, that what was coming fit better than any piece he had forced into that empty place. The wind was cutting through a fog he hadn't realized his foundations were built upon.

"It was after you were born," Elizabeth said. "The first time we all came to know she wasn't right. It was the screaming. She was screaming, screeching like a siren in the night. Aubrey was there too, you know. He was with your father, waist deep in the waves, trying to pull her back." Elizabeth nodded towards Aubrey, as if the proof was in him just standing there.

Aubrey was looking down. He didn't say a word, and that said more than enough.

Elizabeth's voice was calm and even. Slowly, she walked closer to the house. Perhaps, for all her anger, for all her frustration with her great-nephew, she still couldn't yell into such big brown eyes. Or perhaps she knew that an elevated voice could make the knowledge hurt no more than it already would.

"Aubrey was the one that pried you from her arms. He carried you back to shore. You were just a baby, Oliver, only a month old. It's lucky your father was still there then. It was lucky he hadn't left yet, or she might have got it done." Elizabeth shook her head. As if the memory was so terrible she needed to shake the remnants of it from her mind.

"We were here, in this same house. We heard Albert first. Shouting her name into the night. And then—it wasn't long after—the screams came. Aubrey ran out the door first, and I was on his heels. But I tell ya now. We weren't sure what the scene was we'd come upon. For all I disliked your mother, the way those screams cut through the night, I thought, for certain, that something terrible was being done to her. But when I saw it, when I stood on the bank, just down over there"—Elizabeth nodded in the direction where Irene and May had disappeared into the fog—"I saw your mother, already waist deep in the water, and your father with a hold of her nightdress, trying to pull her back to shore. And that nightdress tore." She looked to Aubrey as if expecting him to echo her, to reinforce her.

Aubrey said nothing. He didn't look up.

"When it tore was the only time that she stopped screaming," she said. "She was wading straight back out into the water, with her clothes falling off her, and she was quiet then, and only then."

Elizabeth's gaze had trailed off to somewhere beyond that yard, beyond the argument at hand. She refocused her gaze on her nephew. She didn't look at him in challenge; she wasn't begging for retort. She looked him up and down with pity. She looked at him with something that, for her, resembled love.

"I don't know if I would have stopped her. Aubrey might have tried. Lord knows your father would have. But I don't know if I would have thought stopping her was worth it. But for the fact that she had you in her arms." Elizabeth shook her head again, and her gaze fell back to the patchy grass of the yard. "You weren't a month old. And she had you held to her breast. The swell was calm that night, but it was enough that you'd already gotten wet. You didn't cry though. You didn't make a sound. Oliver Brown, I thought you was already dead." Elizabeth's voice quivered. Her eyes were softer than Oliver had ever seen them.

"You were just a babe, but we already loved you, son. And when we realized she held you there, swaddled in white cloth, ready, willing, wanting, to walk you straight into the water . . . That's when we helped your father stop her."

Elizabeth was dressed in a black dress. It didn't fit her well. It had been worn once before when she was much younger. She'd worn it to her mother's funeral. Now she had a shawl over her shoulders to hide that it hardly fit. Elizabeth moved slowly over to the porch. She walked with a fall to one side, like one hip couldn't quite support her weight as well as the other. She didn't have the sea to blame for her body the way her husband did, but time had passed for her just the same, and fishing houses are as hard to keep as the boats. Her body reminded her of her years with every step.

Elizabeth sat on the stoop where Aubrey had. Aubrey shifted a pace backward.

Oliver still stood atop the step. But now feeling like he was towering above them. He didn't like that feeling.

"Albert was still shouting her name when the nightdress tore. And he kept on calling to her as he grabbed at her through the water. He never did yell at her, and I won't never understand why. He just kept calling to her, as if she might answer him all of a sudden. But a woman like that ain't got any capability of answering." Elizabeth sighed, long and slow. "It wasn't just my Aubrey that went out after her. No sir. By then Dorman had come down the shore, and Clyde Newport as well." She looked at Aubrey. "Bobby Ryan was there that night, wadn't he?"

Aubrey didn't look up, but he nodded his head this time.

"They all went out in the water after her. It took three men to get a hold of her, four to drag her back. Aubrey ripped you from her arms. Lord Jesus did she ever scream when he took you away. I'd run halfway out to 'em. I was standing knee deep when Aubrey handed you over to me. My son." She didn't look at him, but she held a hand to her face. "When I felt you breathing, when I felt your little body moving against mine, I was relieved something terrible. I 'aven't ever felt so much relief as that night."

Oliver's fists were no longer clenched. His veins were no longer filled with the pulsing blood of anger's passion. All that kept him standing had slipped away. He felt like he remained upright because of a coincidence of balance. He wished that it had been a struggle to imagine the scene the way his aunt described it. But her story made far too much sense.

"Why?" He felt himself speaking before he was ready to. "Why did she do that?"

"Oh, we tried to ask her, but she spoke such nonsense. Nothing could be made of it. There weren't much reality in her for a long time." Elizabeth's voice suddenly rose an octave as she continued. "She tried it again, a couple of times. She never made it so far, never even made it to the water before she was stopped. It did stop though. And then she gave it up for a long while. She seemed to be sensible, a proper mother for a spell." Elizabeth looked down and smoothed her dress before suddenly bringing up a hand, as if telling Oliver to stop making assumptions before he'd even formed a thought. "Oh, we was all worried. Especially when Albert got sick and had to leave. It was too soon after those strange times. Too quick for her to be left alone with you. We all knew so. But Albert had said, some sternly, that it'd all be okay. And perhaps it would've been if he'd come back. We all kept a close eye on the pair of ya. But when the letter came, we shouldn't 'ave left her alone."

"We should 'ave asked what she wanted with the water," Aubrey said. Finally deciding it was time to take part in the story.

"We did ask, sure," Elizabeth said.

"Well, ya shouldn't never have taken an answer so easy." Aubrey shook his head. "Cleaning stains out of the old rugs, she said. Said her well was low and she didn't want to waste the fresh water." He hadn't looked at Oliver since the story had begun, and even now he spoke to the porch step, not the boy. "Buckets and buckets," he said. "She carried a bucket down to the beach, and she filled it with water and brought it back up to the house. And we watched her every time. Watched her every time to see if she had gone back to her ways, if she was 'aving one of her fits. But you weren't ever with her. And she never went out past her ankles. So, we left it be. And bucket after bucket she carried back up to her house.

"We should have gone by to check sooner," Elizabeth said. "It never should have been so long! We never should have left it so long!" Her tone and her head both lowered then. "But it was a day and half before I went over with a bit of fish and brewis for 'er." Elizabeth sighed long and deep, like she'd been holding her breath for years, for seventeen of them.

Aubrey stepped forward and placed a hand on Elizabeth's shoulder. He didn't look directly at her, and she didn't look at him. But she reached up and held his hand where it lay on her shoulder.

"I don't know how long you'd been there. From the state of her—she was so cold and stiff and swollen up from the salt water—it'd been all night at least. All night. Your head was only just above the water. Your nose was only just above the water. By the time I got there, you were hardly strong enough to stand." Elizabeth shook her head and swallowed. "You were just a babe, not even a boy, You could barely stand proper as it was. And there you were, in a bathtub filled right to the brim with buckets of salt water, chilled to the bone, those big ol' brown eyes of yours bobbing up and down in the water, struggling to breath." Elizabeth placed her hands on her knees and forced herself up onto feet still swollen from walking in the funeral procession in rarely worn dress shoes. "Miracle. Miracle that you were there for me to pick up out of the water, freezing cold and weaker than a sout'west breeze."

Oliver slowly stepped down off the steps. He wasn't going anywhere, but he no longer had any desire to go inside. Getting changed no longer seemed relevant.

Elizabeth spoke to his back as he continued to walk away.

"What she did to herself is unforgivable, Oliver. But I ain't got no doubt in my mind that she wanted to take you with her. I got no doubt in my mind that she wanted you to drown right alongside her. And that's not somethin' I wanted you to know about your own mother, but it's time you puts away those children's stories. You got to face the reality of who she was."

Oliver kept walking.

He didn't know where he was going. He didn't know why he was walking. But the dense fog in front of him looked like comfort. He wanted it to envelope him. He wanted the grey to hide him, to hold him. He walked nowhere but straight out into the fog.

He had heard a tale, a story of what it all could have been, from a man who was just a stranger when Oliver was just a boy. And even though he'd always known such things couldn't be completely true, to believe in them was comforting. He didn't know if he preferred to know the reality. Knowing changed nothing but how he felt.

The fog swallowed him, and he knew that his aunt and uncle could no longer see him. He took in a deep breath of the low tide's salty air. Memories along the shore are influenced by the stories, and the stories are changed by their telling, and the reality always lies somewhere beneath it all. Oliver knew this. He'd experienced it and wondered now if he could dare hope that reality wasn't quite what he'd been told. He wanted the reality to exist somewhere between the stories he knew. But there was more darkness than hope. It had become hard to believe in anything that wasn't terrible. Oliver had learned, all too well, that reality rarely cared about what he wanted.

Selkie

A mythical creature that resembles a seal when in the ocean but is capable of assuming human form and coming onto land.

When Martin had finished his story of the night Albert and Georgia met, there was a long silence between him and the nine-year-old Oliver. They both stared at the window, gaze shifting between darkness and their own reflections. Neither was pretending to look at the water hoping to see Bobby Ryan make it into the harbour. They were only watching the storm. Martin seemed to have slipped off into the memory of a moment; his mind had fallen into stories of a time past. Oliver was caught up compiling a new image of people he couldn't remember.

"I didn't know she was beautiful," Oliver said, staring at his own reflection in the window.

"Aye. Of course she was, lad. To capture yer father so easy as that. More beautiful than any woman on these shores." Martin smiled at the boy. His teacup was empty. It hung at his side, on a single finger. He stole a glance back over his shoulder at the table and the bottle at its centre.

"Oliver," Elizabeth said, sharp and quick.

He turned to his aunt and she nodded towards Martin.

Oliver didn't understand what was being asked of him until Martin held his empty mug towards him. Oliver took the cup in both hands and walked back over to the table. His aunt turned away before he was at her side. She was making conversation as she held out the bottle, tipping it blindly into the cup.

Oliver's eyes widened as he saw the black liquid rising higher and higher. He glanced between Elizabeth and the pouring bottle. He wanted to say something but was afraid to speak while all the adults were in conversation. Just as the rum was reaching the very brim, she pulled the bottle back. Oliver was relieved at first, but then realized, staring at the overfilled cup, that he had to walk it all the way back to the window.

One foot in front of the other, a gentle laying of the heel, a tender following of the toes. Oliver carried the mug back to the window, cradling the rum as if it were a volatile substance, a mug of aged dynamite waiting to erupt at the slightest knock. The walk back to the window was long.

Martin didn't seem to be aware of the boy's expedition. He took the mug without even looking at him.

"Ta," he said. But only after an audible sip. "It was almost magical ta see, ye know. Albert hadn't shown much in the way of interest to any maid. And more than a couple acceptable young lasses had batted their eyelashes at 'im. But when your mother arrived, he was enchanted. Many folks thought it awful curious how quick he fell."

Oliver marvelled at the idea of such instant affection. He imagined it with the kind of admiration that comes easy to children who hadn't yet loved.

"She was just that beautiful?" He asked with as much awe as curiosity.

"Nay, son. It was more than just beauty that stole yer father's heart. Oh, she was beautiful unlike any other, but she was unlike any other in many a way. She had a look on her face like she was seeing things differently than the rest of us. Or she'd seen it already, just in a different way. She was unlike anything yer father had ever encountered."

"She was so different he fell for her," Oliver said, more confidently.

Martin smiled, but more to himself than towards the boy. "Nay, son. It wasn't just that either." He paused. Words he couldn't quite find, or something he hadn't quite decided upon, hesitated on the tip of his tongue. He sipped his rum again. "Your mother, and her time with your father, always seemed like an old story."

Oliver didn't say anything. He knew so little of his parents that he wouldn't know if his mother was like any stories he'd heard.

"I wouldn't imagine it's a story you'd know too well. It made it over here from my home." Martin gave a nod towards the blackness of the window. "But it's not told the same way anymore. The stories here are of this place, and not that one."

Oliver considered for a moment where the man meant. He had met fishermen from Bonavista. They didn't sound like this man.

"St. John's?" he asked.

Martin chuckled gently. This time his smile was meant for the child. "Nay, lad. An entire ocean and up from Newfoundland. Orkney is where I was a boy."

Oliver had never heard of this place. "Was my mother from there?"

Martin had another nay on his lips, but he hesitated.

"She hadn't ever said so much, but perhaps."

Martin was seeing something past reflections and the view out the window. His thoughts had wandered to his home as he imagined the boy's mother on those shores. The memory of the isles grew clear to him for a moment, and with that recollection came thoughts of his brother. Bobby Ryan was still out there somewhere, on the water. Or under it.

"There's a story of a man," Martin said, searching for distraction in a telling. "A bachelor even more desirable than yer father who fell for a woman who was just as different and beautiful as your mother."

Oliver turned away from the window to look up at Martin.

"Can I hear the story?" he pleaded.

"Perhaps you already have."

Oliver said nothing but he hardly blinked, waiting for Martin to speak.

Martin smiled gently at the anxious child before looking back out the window and taking a deep gulp from his teacup.

"As the story goes, there was a man—the Goodman o' Wastness, they called him—who couldn't be wooed by any maiden up and down the shores, until he met his wife. His wife was something truly special. You see, she wasn't a woman at all. She was a selkie."

"A selkie?" Oliver echoed.

Martin nodded. "That's what they used to call seals in the old tongue, where I come from."

"She was a seal?"

Martin nodded. "A special kind of seal. Selkies and seal folk live in the ocean as seals, ye see. Grey seals, same as the ones ye see here every now and again. But when they come onto land, they can strip away their sealskin and walk about just like men and women."

"Why would they do that?" Oliver couldn't see why a seal would want to leave the ocean.

"Sometimes for love," Martin said. "Sometimes, perhaps, it's just curiosity. I suppose if you were both a seal and a boy, it'd be strange to only ever live as one. You'd feel like part of yerself is trapped inside all the time, don't ye think?"

Oliver shrugged.

"I imagine so. Selkies are always torn you see, between their love for the ocean and their loved ones upon the shore. There's many stories about seal folk, and they're hardly ever happy because they're always longing for one or the other." Martin's smile seemed to have given way under its own weight. The corners of his mouth had dropped; his bottom lip had grown. "As the story goes, the Goodman—who'd never taken a wife—was walking along the shore one day when he saw a pod of selkies laying about, as humans, in the sunshine. They were playing in the sea and resting on the rocks, and every one of them was beautiful. Now, since the Goodman grew up where these stories are plentiful, he knew what they were the moment he saw them. When the selkies saw the Goodman coming, they all dove back into the sea. But one of 'em forgot their sealskin. So the Goodman scooped it up before they could come back for it."

"Because he wanted to be a seal?"

Martin's smile returned for a moment. "No, lad. Because if a selkie doesn't have their skin, then they can't change and return to the ocean."

Oliver frowned in confusion.

"The man took the sealskin so that the selkie wouldn't leave," Martin said. "So they couldn't go back to the sea."

"That doesn't seem very nice."

"Nay. I don't say it was a nice thing to go and do." Martin shook his head. "In the story, the sealskin belonged to a beautiful selkie maiden. She pleads with the Goodman to give her back her skin, and perhaps he was going to return it to her."

Oliver nodded, encouraging the fictional character to act in accordance with the morals of a nine-year-old.

"But when he got to speaking to the selkie woman, the Goodman fell in love with her. Just so quick as a couple words. So he started pleading right back at her, begging her to stay on the land and become his wife. As the story goes, he convinced the selkie maiden. They say that the selkie woman was happy, and that the Goodman treated her well. They had seven children together, and each one was bonnier than any other youngster up and down the shores. But the selkie woman always missed the ocean. She couldn't help but long for the sea."

"But," Oliver said, "didn't they live by the sea? Couldn't she still see it?"

"Aye, she could. But it's different to live beside the water than to live within it. I imagine it's hard, to look at what you love and not be able to be with it. Maybe even harder than not seeing it at all." Martin tightened his grip on his cup as if trying to squeeze more rum from the ceramic.

"Well, I think I would still rather see it," Oliver said confidently.

"Love and longing change with time. Sometimes things get harder, instead of easier. Whenever her husband was away, the selkie woman would search their house for where he hid the sealskin. One day, while she was looking, one of their daughters saw the frantic search, and she told her mother that she knew where such a sealskin was, not knowing why her mother sought it. When the selkie woman found her sealskin, she cried with joy and kissed her children goodbye. She ran straight to the ocean before her husband could return. She put on her sealskin and jumped in the water. Then the goodman's wife turned back into a seal and swam away, never to be seen again."

After a long pause, Oliver asked, "Did her husband miss her?"

"Oh, terribly." Martin sighed quietly and continued more softly. "They say that he wandered up and down the beach every day, all alone, hoping to see her again."

"Did she miss her husband?" Oliver looked up at Martin.

"Of course, but not so much as she had missed the sea when she was with him."

Oliver looked at his feet, not wanting to see Martin's expression. "But what about her children?"

"Oh, she missed them too."

Oliver frowned. No one in the story seemed to be happy in the end.

Martin saw the boy's perplexed expression and took another sip of his rum. "There are many stories like that one," he said.

Oliver said nothing. He wasn't sure he wanted to hear another.

"In some stories, the selkie takes her children back to sea with her."

"Really?" Oliver's face brightened for a moment.

"In some stories, selkies give their lovers on land lots of gold to take the child away." Martin hesitated. He chewed his tongue for a moment before swallowing. "But sometimes the selkies carry the children as babies out into the sea with them. Never to be seen again."

Oliver looked away from Martin, back at the black window. The idea of the children getting to return to the sea with their selkie parent was exciting to him, but the children leaving forever didn't seem happy.

"Are the selkie people good?" he asked.

Martin's head tilted to the side for a moment. There was a

tightness to his lips, as if they were holding in all the words he wouldn't say. "That depends on the story, lad. And it depends on who's hearing it."

Oliver was silent for a long moment. Correctness being dependent on perspective was a concept he was still too young to have considered. But he was too polite to express his confusion and lacked enough confidence to ask another question.

"There are kind stories of the seal folk. Stories of them remembering good deeds done to them and returning them years later. Stories of them saving fishermen who can't swim. And along these shores, I've heard stories about their strength and kindness. Folks here tell stories of them as loving parents, and as the best of workers.

"Selkies are always strangers here, showing up on the shore from nowhere, coming and going on their own time, indifferent to boats and tides. Folks don't often say it aloud, but I've heard 'em say things like that about yer mother. Folks say that she stepped right out of the ocean, and out of a sealskin, the night she met your father. I imagine you'll hear those stories too, one day . . . Or hear all the worse." Martin lowered his voice to only a whisper. "And perhaps you'll decide that them sayin' she was a selkie isn't such a bad thing after all."

"Was she?" Oliver asked.

Martin smiled. "Perhaps, lad. Or perhaps that's just what folks say." Before Oliver could protest the vague answer, Martin drained the last of his teacup and held the mug out to the boy.

By the time Oliver had returned to the window with another cup, overfilled with rum, the storytelling had passed. Martin silently took the cup from him and didn't look away from the darkness beyond the window.

Oliver looked out the window too, quietly waiting, hoping another story would start. In the silence, he became caught up in what he'd learned. His face grew troubled.

Oliver finally spoke. "What if the selkie never gets its skin back?"

Martin turned towards the boy.

"What if the person from land who took the sealskin hid it too well, or what if something happened to them?" Oliver spoke to the window glass, unwilling to look at Martin.

Martin held his silence, waiting for Oliver to turn to him.

Oliver's chin was tucked against his chest and his face burned. He was embarrassed by his question and didn't want to look at Martin.

Martin matched the boy's stance and looked back out the window. "A selkie unable to return to the ocean is no different than a man unable to return to shore," he said. "They'll last as long as they can. But eventually, they'll drown."

Martin looked at the reflection of Oliver's sad face. He thought of Sule Skerry and other tales to tell the child. Tales that may not end any happier, but at least ones that were further away.

Lore

Traditional knowledge or belief, often tied to place.

After the day of his grandmother's funeral, Oliver and Aunt Elizabeth rarely exchanged words. A sadness had found Oliver, deeper than the disappointment left by any child's cruel words or the sorrow of the exclusion he'd experienced his entire life. The sadness that crashed over him after that day took the shine from his eyes. Oliver himself didn't change, but the way he thought of himself did. Perhaps all that had kept him content, kept him above the harshness of those around him, were the possibilities hidden in the unknown. In not knowing his past, his blood, he'd had a story that was all his own. After that day, however, Oliver realized that his story had been started and tainted long before he was old enough to be aware of it. He was now old enough to realize that what he'd gone through, the way he had been treated his whole life, wasn't fair, and that he was allowed to be upset by it.

As uncomfortable as Oliver had grown with the town, as much as he felt that he didn't belong in his home, he knew of no other. He didn't have anywhere to go. He had no money or skills, and few people would offer him work to gain experience either.

Oliver was tied to a place that he no longer wanted to be a part of, a place that had never offered him a part to be.

He found temporary escapes in any way he could. He would walk the coastline and the trails that surround the harbour, distancing himself from other people, always staying close to the comfort of the ocean. In the following months, Oliver came to be known by his lonesome silhouette, standing like a statue on the oceanside cliffs or walking the beaches. On those walks, he would fantasize about the ocean's vastness. Not just that of the sea he had watched doing battle with the rocks for his entire life, but of the ocean beyond the sightline of land. He hoped he could escape to the sea one day, that a captain would take him as crew. He fantasized about how long he could avoid needing to return to a port.

The Newports' story had swept across Salvage quickly in the days following the rescue of their boat. Most folks around the harbour disregarded it. They attributed it to the make-and-break, or to the delirium of seasick sailors. But this didn't keep eyebrows from being raised. Even those who doubted if Oliver was even there that day turned a little further from him when he walked down to the wharves in the morning. No one seemed to want to talk to him. At the least, they didn't want to be seen talking to him.

He found what work he could. Helping his uncle mostly, repairing nets and fixing bait traps. He'd asked on many occasions to join his uncle on the water, to help man his skiff. But Aubrey already had a crew and claimed he didn't need another hand. Oliver knew there were men who didn't want to be in a boat with him. They were wary of him, as if being on the water with him might bring some strange misfortune. There was a time when Oliver would have had all the work he needed in the salting and drying of the fish. It was shore work that could be done in solitude. But with fish plants opening in every other harbour along the shore, there was less work even in flaking fish these days. And Oliver was at the bottom of the list of those who got the work.

He'd considered walking down the shore to the sawmill that Martin Ryan owned. He believed that Martin held a sympathy for him and would have offered him work, but Oliver knew he wasn't built for that kind of labour. His hands were too soft, and he had no eye for good lumber, nor any knack for straight cuts. It was the sea that Oliver belonged to, and he promised himself that he would ask for passage on every merchant ship that came through the harbour. And if that didn't work, he'd make his way to Bonavista and try there instead.

When he was a child, Oliver had gained companionship from being near the water. The smell of salt in the air, the cool mist off a breaking wave . . . That had been enough company to soothe his aching heart. But now the water was tainted to him; it was a force that carried a capacity for evil. The sea was more like a person to him now. No matter how much he loved it, he couldn't forget what it was capable of doing. That sea had taken his mother, and it would have taken him as well. Even if it was an end that she'd chosen, he couldn't help but feel her loneliness inside him. He didn't know what she'd looked like, and for once, he was happy for that. It meant he couldn't be haunted by a mental image of her slipping under the water. But that didn't stop him from imagining the burning in her lungs as her body begged for air. No matter how badly she may have wanted to go, Oliver couldn't imagine it had been a good departure.

The water still comforted Oliver Brown, but it no longer washed away all his sadness. It no longer held all his loneliness at bay.

It had hardly been four months since the argument with his aunt. Summer, the season always short on these shores, had come and gone. Autumn had arrived a few weeks back: the sun didn't cut through the clouds the same way, and the wind-driven storms that track up from the south were lasting longer. Fall fish are sweet though, and the fishermen continued laying their nets in hopes of beating quotas and making better winters for themselves.

A southwesterly breeze, warm and even, was coming off the shore. There was a large swell on. Although the local weather was calm, the winds well offshore must have been strong. The sea rolled so high that a wind from any other direction would have made for dangerous work. It would have kept many boats at port. But there is safety in the southwesterly. The warm wind coming off the land could never gain the momentum and power of a gust from the north. Such a gust can track for miles, uninterrupted, and pick up the sea with it as it blows.

Oliver had his back to the wind. It wrapped around his body as if gently nudging him closer to the edge of the cliff, encouraging him towards the water far below. His black, curly hair hadn't been cut in a long time; it was caught in the wind and blew around his face. He stood on a familiar peak, high above the water, looking out at the fishing boats hauling in their catch. From this distance, the boats could barely be deciphered from one another. But knowing the fishing grounds and where which nets and traps were placed allowed Oliver to know, more or less, who was who. The waters rolled in high and heavy, and the boats bobbed up and down, almost out of sight from each other when they were at the bottom of the swell.

Oliver felt it first in the stillness. He noticed that there was no longer a breeze against his back. There was a stillness he recognized just as it was disappearing. As if erupting from the water itself, a blast of wind came over the cliff face and blew his hair out of his face. The breeze twisted around him as the winds were turning. A firm gust came again, northeasterly, straight in from the sea.

Oliver looked down at the boats; many were partway through hauling nets. They weren't far offshore, and even with the winds coming up, they had time to make it to the safety of ports. They'd finish their hauls and come in. Some might push it if there wasn't yet sight of any cloud's headland. If black mountains weren't rolling through the sky, the fishermen might try to bring in another catch. Fish weren't as good as they once were, and the price was only worse. But most would cut their losses for the day, and sail in to secure their boats.

When Oliver was a boy, the storms used to inspire an excitement. The sheer power of the wind as it whipped the ocean into a state of frothing fury was a spectacle to behold. As he got older, that excitement was replaced with concern. After Bobby Ryan failed to return, Oliver realized the danger of the water. As he grew older still, that worry was replaced with acceptance. The nature of a livelihood pulled from the sea meant that sometimes the sea would pull back. Caution and preparation kept men safe, and danger could usually be calculated. Now, as the turning winds of a coming autumn storm swept over him, he was neither excited nor afraid. The storm would come with or without his concern, and if he let it, would bring its own emotions too.

Oliver Brown had no reason to believe that anything was different about that storm. Nor did any of the fishermen. There had been no red sky in the morning, and the swell that was present seemed softer than yesterday, not building. No fishermen had whistled in their boat on the way out the harbour: no traditions had been skipped, no signs ignored. But the storm that was brewing would be greater than most inhabitants of the harbour had ever seen.

All great storms come with stories. Sometimes the stories of the storms are fierce enough to define a season. Some storms are grand enough to mark an entire year—time and work defined by what there was before the storm and what there was after. But still other storms will mark a decade. Waves will remake beaches, winds will undo forests, and storm surges will carve away at embankments and anything humans had built upon them. Some storms, a community will spend years recovering from, and they will separate an entire era into before and after. Oliver had no way of knowing that most of his life had taken place in a before.

As the boats began making their way back into port, Oliver also turned from the cliff face and made his way back to the harbour. By the time skiffs had docked and fish were unloaded, the force of what was coming was growing clear. It took only an hour for the waves to begin washing over the wharves. The sky had grown dark; clouds seemed not just to be rolling in but to be taking form in the thin air of the blue sky above.

For all of Oliver's exclusion, no one refused his help at the harbour that day. Boats without sheltered berths were pulled ashore. Those left in the water were given an extra line, and then another line still. Bow and stern ropes weren't strong enough to be trusted.

At first the town worked methodically, preparing for just another bout of bad weather, but as the rain began to pour, the work grew more frantic. It wasn't just the boats, the townspeople soon realized. The windows of houses would need to be barricaded and sealed. Already the trunks of fir trees were being tested. Sheets of water swept across the waves, pounding the ocean's surface with such vengeance that the line between ocean and sky had blurred.

Even if the following events hadn't transpired, the storm would have been spoken about for years to come. Wharves would be destroyed, boats washed under. Any fishing net left at sea would come to be tossed onto the shore as the ocean roared. But for all the damage that storm would cause, the story it would leave behind would outlast the repercussions of its power.

Oliver was standing at his uncle's wharf when Aubrey made it into the harbour. Wordlessly, Aubrey nodded towards the slip. He wouldn't risk the boat he'd built to the wind and waves. He'd pull her high and dry until the storm had passed. Oliver worked silently beside his uncle, securing the gear and carrying the catch up from the water. When their own livelihood was taken care of, they went to their neighbours, helping others prepare.

Oliver was kneeling at the edge of a wharf, tying another aft line around a cleat, when he took the time to scan the harbour. A quick count of the boats, and the berths, seeing that all was in place. Oliver was amongst the first to notice the absence of a skiff. Before he asked, before he even checked the numbers on the boats pulled onto the slipways, he knew which vessel wasn't there.

"Aubrey!"

Oliver heard his uncle's name called and turned to see Clarke Genge walking towards them. He knew Clarke only from a distance. Since the day on the ice pans all those years ago, Clarke had spoken to him only once, if it could be called that: when he saw Oliver with his son in the graveyard. Oliver stood up as he approached. Clarke glanced past Aubrey to where he stood. Once, Oliver would have avoided the man's eyes. He would have bowed his head and turned away. But as the rain pounded them, Oliver's back remained straight, his jaw set. He watched as the man approached, wanting to see him speak to ensure that he understood him over the wind.

Clarke called out to Aubrey. "Did you see where the b'ys are to?" He was out of breath. Aubrey wasn't the first fisherman he'd been asking.

"No, my son." Aubrey shook his head. He spoke gently.

Oliver watched Clarke swallow at the response. He gave a brief nod.

"But the swell was some high." Aubrey's voice rose an octave, trying to pull spirits up with it. "You couldn't get a proper eyeline on anyone. They could 'ave been right behind me for all I could tell."

Clarke nodded a little firmer then. He had hardly stopped walking, and as soon as Aubrey confirmed that he didn't know, began walking the shoreline again, on to the next fishermen. Now he was looking for information. Soon he would be looking for hope and, eventually, only for comfort.

Just before Clarke reached the next wharf and Aubrey and Oliver had returned to their work, Clarke looked back towards them, for just a moment, but at Oliver instead of Aubrey. Oliver's face was painted with his own concern. The two locked eyes for a moment, and then Clarke gave Oliver the slightest nod before continuing on.

It's hard to guess what Clarke Genge had been thinking in that moment. Perhaps he had forgotten all about that day in the graveyard. Or maybe his worry for his son outweighed the petty contempt he had for Oliver. Perhaps he saw the concern on Oliver's face and knew they shared a fear. Or maybe Clarke was thinking back to that day on the ice pans and the worry he'd had for his child, and the relief he'd had when another child saved him.

Aubrey looked back at Oliver as Clarke walked away. He nodded to the boy and then knelt to finish tying the bowline. Oliver knelt and finished securing the aft.

Johnathan and Rebecca had gotten engaged over the summer. They were set to be married anytime now. Oliver didn't know the date. He hadn't been invited and hadn't tried to listen when it was spoken about, telling himself he was indifferent to it. He'd anticipated the wedding for a year at least, and although the thought of it still caused a tightening in his chest and a twisting of his stomach so hard that it hurt, he'd learned to keep his thoughts from wandering to it.

The impending wedding was why Johnathan was on the water at that moment. Clarke had helped his son build his first motorboat over the last winter, knowing he'd be marrying a girl in the coming year. He'd wanted his son to be able to earn his own living for his family. He'd wanted to give him the best he could. Johnathan was a fair sailor, a smart lad and even stronger than he was bright. But he was young. He was barely a man and now in charge of a boat. Even if only an open fishing boat, it left him responsible for the lives of the two other men aboard it. Now Gary Matchim and Clayton Saunders were more than just Johnathan's friends, but his crewmates as well.

Something Oliver had heard his aunt say long ago echoed in his head. "There's a fifth thing that will never say 'enough': young fishermen. And you don't get to be an old fisherman if you don't learn to be satisfied."

Oliver kept his eye on the harbour mouth as he finished tying off the neighbour's boat.

The men were all heading inside now. Hunkering down to last out the storm. Eyes were still on the open water, waiting for another boat to come in. Word travelled fast that Johnathan Genge and his crew weren't accounted for. A harbour during a storm is not unlike barracks in wartime. There's a roll call, and if a name isn't answered, heads hang low but no one suggests going out to look. No boat in that harbour could offer them any help. To go back out would only be putting others in danger. It'd be too difficult to fight to stay afloat to try and give any aid. It would be a night of tea and prayers, and Oliver had yet to see either of those help anything.

Oliver dragged his feet as he followed Aubrey back up to the house. With each step, he let his uncle slip a little further ahead. He kept looking back towards the harbour mouth, hoping to catch a glimpse of a white boat amongst whitecapped waves. He stole glances at his uncle and then at the far side of the house, away from the door and towards the trails that traced the shoreline. Oliver let his direction drift towards the far end of the house until he was walking at an angle to Aubrey.

He couldn't go inside yet. He couldn't sit in the house and stare out a window they'd scarcely keep open for fear of debris. Oliver, knowing Johnathan was out there—wet and cold and fighting to survive—would rather feel the storm on his skin than feel the warmth of the woodstove.

When Aubrey was almost at the door, Oliver began striding to the other end of the house, intending to slip away and head back to the same perch he had occupied earlier, on the cliff high above. Despite the battering he'd receive from the storm, he would go there and hope it gave him the best chance of seeing Johnathan's boat. He had to try and see, even if he'd only be able to watch helplessly.

Oliver was caught in the thought of this, of seeing without being able to do anything. As he was realizing how deeply every fibre of him wanted to be able to do something, his uncle called out.

"Oliver." Hardly loud enough to ensure he'd cover the distance between them.

He stopped and turned to his uncle.

Stone still, Aubrey stood with one hand on the doorknob.

They both said nothing for a long moment. Oliver wasn't going to go into the house and didn't want to try and explain why. He didn't have a valid explanation and feared what he would say if asked to justify his decision.

Aubrey let go of the doorknob. Wordlessly, he walked over to the corner of the house where Oliver was waiting. He looked directly at his nephew as he walked, taking in Oliver's face. He seemed to absorb every inch of his appearance, as if trying to compile the most accurate image, before he finally met Oliver's eyes.

Oliver wasn't sure what he expected from his uncle. Part of him anticipated being reprimanded. Another part of him was waiting for the words "there's nothing you can do" to come off the man's lips.

But Aubrey reached out and grabbed Oliver's shoulder.

Oliver realized that the man's face was wet with more than rain, and the tremble in his lip had nothing to do with the cold.

"Be safe, son," he said, his voice barely more than a whisper. "Goodbye." Aubrey squeezed his shoulder, hard and firm, and turned away, lowering his head and watching his feet as he walked away. He didn't look back as he stepped into the house.

Oliver told himself he didn't understand why Aubrey was so upset. He told himself he couldn't afford to worry about it, not when all his concern was caught up in considering the water and the winds that were corrupting it. But perhaps part of him was already coming to understand.

Oliver turned away from his aunt and uncle's house, the only home he had ever known but not one he'd ever considered his own. With head down and shoulders hunched, he marched against the wind and the rain back to the heights of the cliff. The rocks were slippery and he fell, more than once, as he clambered over them. The trees bent and whipped and creaked; the storm tested the forest as he walked through it. Oliver didn't consider stopping or turning back. There was nothing he could do, but this felt like he was doing something. This effort just to see was at least an output of effort. He had to stand up there and look.

But trying was all that proved possible. The storm raged with such force that it swept away the view. The shore was consumed by ocean spray and crashing waves; the rolling swells were all crested white and battered by sheets of rain. Even where the rain was falling softer, the fog had laid out thick fingers. The sea was in turmoil as the sky raged.

Oliver, his legs apart and knees bent just to stand against the weather, stood at the cliff's very edge as the rain and wind whipped around him. He toed the sheer rock that dropped away to seas that boomed and echoed over the wind. It could be suggested that he wasn't aware of how close he was to the edge, that he didn't realize how precariously he was balanced. Or that he was entirely aware and filled with fear, but the closer he was to the edge, the better his chances were of seeing something in the distance.

Perhaps it wasn't fear at all. Perhaps Oliver Brown stood at the edge not despite the danger but because of it. Maybe he was prepared to not see the boat—or worse, prepared to see it capsized, too far out for there to be any hope. And maybe he stood on the cliff's edge not in defiance of the drop, but in preparation for it. Perhaps that's the way his story would come to end.

Through the screaming winds and thundering waves—and the depth of Oliver's thoughts—a soft sound somehow found him.

It came twice before he even realized it was there. A sound

that was not akin to the storm's chaos. The third time, he heard his name. "Oliver!"

It didn't come from the ocean below, where he hoped for signs of human life. It came from behind him. He stepped back from the edge, careful to keep his balance, and turned around to see the sodden and struggling form of Rebecca Smith, fighting her way across the clifftop towards him. The simple dress she wore was muddy and torn by tree branches. Her chest heaved and Oliver could tell it was from crying as much as it was exertion.

Rebecca, even now, fails to find an answer as to what led her to the clifftop. The entire night is blurred to her, but its events are a part of her. A moment in time so drenched in emotions she can never forget it, yet she can never remember it clearly. *Desperation* is the one word she returns to when she tells the story of that night. She was desperate and willing to cling to anything, no matter how ridiculous, that could ease that sensation of despair. Anything that could, for a moment, give her some kind of hope.

"Oliver. Oliver Brown!" she called again, not managing to even look towards him as she fought her way through the winds.

Oliver watched as she fell to her knees, her soft hands catching herself on the rocks. The same sensation Oliver always felt when he saw her washed over him. Even as he pitied her struggling on the rocks, he felt his stomach twist and turn. His mind, saturated for months in sadness and now so consumed by concern, was seared with the closest thing to anger he had ever known. He didn't know why she had come here, why she had interrupted the solace he sought in the storm. He could feel his frustration rippling across his skin. It was her fault Johnathan was out there at all, so he wanted to blame it on her, somehow. He wanted to blame someone.

But she didn't rise from her knees. She couldn't fight against the wind to get her feet beneath her weight and balance on the wet rocks. Her hands were bright red with the wet and cold, and she shook from the chill and the tears. She tried again and again to stand back up.

Despite everything else Oliver felt, kindness was at his core. Despite his frustration and sadness and jealousy, kindness was too integral a part of his nature to ever be overcome by lesser feelings. Making his way to where Rebecca had fallen, he used his body to block her face from the wind. He was protecting her from a force of nature, the way her betrothed had once pretended to do for him. He put an arm over her shoulder and gently helped her to stand.

Rebecca was crying with such fierceness she was almost hysterical.

"You shouldn't be out here." He sounded colder than he intended, but softness held no place in the storm.

She cowered close to him and his protection from the wind and cried desperately. "Oliver," she said, "help." Her voice was slight, as if it were failing.

"You're okay," he said, more softly than before.

Rebecca shook her head against his chest. "Help him," she said.

Oliver realized then what had driven her there. In that moment, he understood the depth of her love because he understood the depth of her desperation. She had tossed aside reason. The thought of losing someone who meant so much to her was something she couldn't bear. She would sooner succumb to a fantasy than accept a reality without Johnathan. Logic was no longer of importance. She needed only to do everything she possibly could.

Oliver was going to say there was nothing he could do. He was going to apologize to Rebecca and tell her that no one could do anything. But she knew that, and Oliver knew that she knew that. How could she not? How could she possibly think anything different? Rebecca was a smart girl and a strong one. She had the kind of fierceness that was needed to outlast hard times, the strength of character it takes to survive the longest winters. The tears on her face, the hysteria that had found her were the product of a love too grand to be governed by sensibilities.

"Help him," she said, and pounded her fists on his shoulders.

Oliver said nothing. His face was still and sad as he looked down at her.

Perhaps it was the silence. Perhaps it was the cover from the storm his body provided. Whatever it may have been, something allowed Rebecca to take a deep breath. She looked down at the uneven rock they stood upon and exhaled through pursed lips, calming her crying.

When she turned back up to him, she was the person Oliver knew. She was the child who had tested the ice pans almost as much as he and Johnathan had. She was the girl who hadn't joined in his teasing. The storyteller who never told tales of him or his mother. She was the woman who loved Johnathan, not the one who'd stolen him. Just the one who was lucky enough to receive his love. Oliver saw her then as a product of the sea, not so different from himself. She had been raised in the smell of salt water and had grown up accepting the fragility of life.

It wasn't desperation so much as determination that she spoke through then. "I've seen how you look at him," she said.

Oliver looked away.

"I've caught you watching him. You look at him like I do." She reached up and grabbed Oliver's face, turning it towards her own. "And I've seen him look at you too. I don't know what passed between youse. I know he won't never tell me. But I knows you love him. And I know part of him loves you too." Fresh tears converged with raindrops and flooded her cheeks.

Oliver's chest throbbed and heat swelled across his cheeks.

"There's nothing we can do," he said.

Her free hand pounded his chest again.

"If anyone can do something, it's you, Oliver Brown." She let go of his face, and both her hands grabbed at the front of his shirt. "I saw you save him before. I was right there, and I don't care what people says. There was no miracle. There was just you." Her hands were balled into fists, clenching his clothing. "It's not for me. You can 'ave him. Just don't let 'im die out there. Don't let him be drowned."

Oliver wiped away tears with the back of his hand. He knew that Johnathan being his was a proposal more impossible than him being saved from the sea.

"There's nothing I can do," Oliver said, hardly loud enough for it to be heard over the storm. Rebecca's eyes met his. He saw her chest heave as she bit her bottom lip, trying to hold in a gasping teary breath. She nodded at him.

"Of course not," she finally said. "I'm sorry. I don't know what I was thinking."

Rebecca held on to Oliver for a long moment, not breaking their eye contact until, finally, he turned and looked back out towards the ocean. "I know that you'd save him if you could," she said. "I know." She let go of Oliver and walked back to the start of the trail, shooting back only a fleeting glance before disappearing back into the trees.

Oliver was left standing alone out there above the ocean, in the heart of all the storm's rage.

~

No one can say for certain what transpired thereafter. Rebecca joined Johnathan's family in the warmth of their house. They all comforted each other and passed around false hope. Aubrey and Elizabeth stayed up most the night, telling each other that it was because they couldn't sleep through the storm. Elizabeth had said nothing when she saw her husband's cheeks wet. Aubrey had said nothing when he left his wife sitting in sad silence, alone at the kitchen table.

The storm raged—worse, they would all come to claim, than any storm they had ever seen. When they'd tell stories of the storm in years to come, the skies would sound like nothing less than an act of God. The sea would sound like a malevolent god all itself. Wharves were torn apart, and the roofs of houses were pulled away. Boats not pulled to dry land were smashed upon the shores they once considered home, and even some of the vessels that sat on slips had been dragged back into the water to meet their demise.

Countless people around the town would claim to have seen a light through the storm. Or they would say they'd heard an unnatural sound after the storm had passed. Some folks would claim to have been visited by one of the lost sailors—Johnathan himself, or one of his crew mates. People would testify that kettles boiled without stoves being lit, that nonexistent alleys rolled down stairs, that doors were knocked upon without visitors. The Old Hag made many rounds that night, or so the people would claim. Countless different versions of what had taken place were told thereafter. Some dying quick, others likely outlasting the truth, whatever that truth was.

The storm ended as quickly as it came. The air was still in the morning. Even the seas had calmed. The water, which had caused such chaos hours before, met the blue morning sky like a mirror.

Birds chirped in chorus amongst toppled trees. The destruction of the storm was astonishing once revealed by the new day. No boats could break the serenity of the morning after. The sea had tossed anything belonging to humankind back onto the shore.

Rebecca went to Aubrey and Elizabeth's house the next afternoon. She went to see Oliver, perhaps to apologize—or maybe, even then, she knew she was going to say thank you. But Aubrey told her, with tight lips and damp eyes, that Oliver hadn't come home.

For Rebecca, who keeps the surname of her late husband, a man who died after some fifty years of happy marriage, there are two simple truths of that storm that should always be told. She doesn't offer them as explanation. They're just two happenings that Rebecca Genge takes upon herself to tell.

That morning, with no memory, no sign of their vessel and no explanation of their salvation, all three fishermen—Clayton, Gary and Johnathan—were found alive on the beach, in the safety of Salvage Harbour. And Oliver Brown was never seen again.

A young man always kinder than his upbringing should have made him. Always capable of more than people thought should be possible. His life had been so steeped in what others believed to be beyond natural that to the day those three men died—decades later, grown old, in their beds—they openly thanked him for their lives.

Perhaps it's a collective guilt that buried the retelling of this story. Or perhaps it's the slow decay of belief in superstition. Whatever the case may be, some still say that—if you're lucky—you might see a seal in Salvage.

Acknowledgements

Thank you to my parents, Barb and Clay, and my sister and brother- in-law, Rebecca and Dan, for their endless support and continuous faith in my writing.

Thank you to Bree, and to all my friends and partners both present and past, who gave me relentless encouragement. Unconditional love is rare, but it is fundamental to humanity.

Thank you to Lisa for her belief in this story's potential from its first pages.

Thank you to my substantive editor, Samanda, for the structure she offered my creativity. Our childhood friendship has come so far. Thank you to my copy editor, Shelley, for all her patience and careful guidance.

Thank you to Alex, and to Mihalis, for being constantly willing to help, encourage, and tell me when I'm wrong. We all need that.

Thank you to the entire team at Breakwater Books for putting their faith in this story and in me.

Thank you to so many passionate professors who bettered me. Thank you to the whole team at the Memorial University of Newfoundland Folklore and Language Archive for helping me to find the stories that built this book.

Thank you to my hometown. While all the characters in this book are fictional, they were inspired by the people I once knew and grew up alongside of.

Thank you to my grandparents, the first storytellers in my life. I hope Dorman will get to read this book. To Jack and Dorothy, who I wish could have seen it in print.

And of course, to my late grandmother Stella, whose voice echoes throughout this entire story.

CLAYTON B. SMITH is a writer from outport Newfoundland, currently residing in St. John's. He has a joint honours degree in English and Philosophy and a diploma in Creative Writing from Memorial University. His writing has appeared in various literary magazines, including *Riddle Fence* and *Paragon*. Clayton's life revolves around people, pints, and prose, in no particular order.